The

and

by the same author

RECIPES FROM AN OLD FARMHOUSE

THE ADVENTURES OF SAM PIG

THE CHRISTMAS BOX

MAGIC WATER

SAM PIG AND HIS FIDDLE

SAM PIG AND THE HURDY-GURDY MAN

THE MAY QUEEN

SAM PIG AND THE DRAGON

SAM PIG'S TROUSERS

SAM PIG AND THE WIND

SAM PIG AND THE SCARECROW

SAM PIG AND THE CHRISTMAS PUDDING

SAM PIG AND THE CUCKOO CLOCK

SAM PIG GOES TO THE THEATRE

LAVENDER SHOES: Eight Tales of Enchantment

THE WEATHER COCK

and other tales

ALISON UTTLEY

Illustrated by Nancy Innes

LONDON · BOSTON

First published in 1945
by Faber and Faber Limited
3 Queen Square London WC1N 3AU
Reprinted in 1949
This paperack edition first published in 1989

Printed in Great Britain by
Richard Clay Ltd Bungay Suffolk

A CIP record for this book is available from
the British Library

ISBN 0-571-14174-9

Contents

Mrs. Mimble and Mr. Bumble Bee

In nearly the smallest house in the world lived Mrs. Mimble, a brown field mouse. She had bright peeping eyes and soft silky reddish hair, which she brushed and combed each morning when she got out of bed. She was a widow, for her husband went to market one night for some corn, and never returned. Old Mr. Toad said he had met Wise Owl on the way. This made Mrs. Mimble nervous, and a loud sound would startle her so much she would lock her door and go to bed.

There was only one room in the nearly-smallest house, and that was the kitchen. Here Mrs. Mimble did her cooking and sewing, but on wash-day she rubbed her linen in the dew and spread it out on the violet leaves to dry. In a corner of the kitchen was a bed, and above it ticked a dandelion clock. In another corner was a wardrobe, and there hung her best red dress edged with fur, and her bonnet and shawl, and the white bow she wore on her breast.

The house was built under a hedge, among the leaves. Its chimney reached the bottom bell of the tall foxglove, which overshadowed the little dwelling like a great purple tree. Mrs. Mimble could put her head out of the kitchen window and listen to the bees' orchestra in the mottled flowers. She dearly loved a tune, and she hummed to the bees as she went about her work. Her house was so cleverly hidden, no one would notice it. Even the tiny spiral of smoke from her chimney disappeared among the foxglove leaves like blue mist, and left only the smell of woodruff in the air.

Farther on, separated from her home by a wild-rose bush, was the very smallest house in the world.

There lived Mr. Bumble Bee. He also had only one room, but it was so little, and so crowded with furniture, it was lucky he could fly, for he never could have walked through his very little door at the end of the passage.

Mr. Bumble was a stout furry bee, with such a big voice that when he talked his pots rattled, and the little copper warming-pan which hung on the wall often fell down with a clatter. So he usually whispered indoors, and sang loudly when he was out in the open where nothing could be blown down. The trees and bushes were too firmly rooted for that.

He was a merry old bachelor, and it was quite natural that he and gentle Mrs. Mimble should be great friends.

All through the winter the little neighbours were very quiet. Mr. Bumble Bee felt so drowsy he seldom left his bed. He curled himself up in the blankets, pulled the bracken quilt over his head, and slept. His fire went out, but the door was tightly shut, and he was quite warm. Now and then he awoke and stretched his arms and legs. He fetched a little honey from his store of honey-pots in the passage and had a good meal. He drank a cup of honey-dew, and then got back to bed again.

Mrs. Mimble was asleep in her house, too. The wind howled and gusts of hail beat against the door.

Snow covered the ground with its deep white eiderdown, and Mrs. Mimble opened her eyes to look at the unexpected brightness at the small window. She jumped out of bed and had a dinner of wheaten bread from the cupboard; but the cold made her shiver, and she crept back under her blankets and brown silk quilt.

Sometimes, when she felt restless, she sat in her chair, rocking, rocking, to the scream of the north wind. Sometimes she opened the door and went out to look for holly berries and seeds, but she never stayed long. Sometimes she pattered to the Bumble Bee's house, but the smallest house in the world was tightly shut, and she returned to bed for another sleep. No smoke came from the neighbouring chimneys; there were no busy marketings in the wood and orchard, no friendly gossips on the walls. All the very wee folk, the butterflies, bees, and ants, were resting.

One morning a bright shaft of sunlight shone straight through the window on to the mouse's bed, and a powder of hazel pollen blew under the door and settled on Mrs. Mimble's nose. She sneezed, Atishoo! and sprang up.

"Whatever time is it? Have I overslept? Catkin and pussy willow out, and I in bed?"

She washed her face in the walnut basin, and brushed her glossy hair. Then she put on her brown dress with the fur cuffs, and pinned a white ribbon to her breast.

"I must pop out and look at the world," said she to herself. "Are the snowdrops over, I wonder?"

She reached down her bonnet and shawl, opened wide her window, and set off.

Mr. Bumble's door was fast shut, and although she knocked until her knuckles were sore, no sound came from the smallest house, and no smoke came from the chimney.

The sun shone down and warmed Mrs. Mimble's back, and she laughed as she ran up the hill.

"Soon he will wake, and won't I tease him!" she chuckled.

She crept under a tall narrow gate into the orchard on the hillside. Over the wall hung clusters of white rock, heavy with scent, and among the flowers sang a chorus of honey-bees.

"Bumble is getting lazy," said Mrs. Mimble. "He ought to be up and out now," but the bees took no notice. They were far too busy collecting honey for their hive in a corner of the orchard to listen to a field mouse.

Under the wall was a bed of snowdrops. They pushed up their green spear-like leaves and held the white drops in veils of green gauze. Mrs. Mimble wrinkled her small nose as she ran from one to another, sniffing the piercingly sweet smell of spring. In a corner a company of flowers was out, wearing white petticoats and green embroidered bodices. Mrs. Mimble sat up on her hind legs and put out a paw to stroke them. The bells shook at her gentle touch, and rang a peal, "Ting-a-ling-spring-a-ling".

She turned aside and ran up the high wall to the white rock and gathered a bunch for Mr. Bumble Bee, to the honey-bees' annoyance.

"Let him get it himself," they grumbled.

Then down she jumped, from stone to stone, and hunted for coltsfoot in the orchard to make herb-beer.

Time had slipped away, and the sun was high when she neared home. A fine smoke, which only her sharp eyes could spy, came from Mr. Bumble's chimney. The door was wide open, and a crackly sound and a loud Hum-m-m-m came from within as the Bumble Bee cleaned his boots and chopped the sticks.

There was no doubt Mr. Bumble was very wide awake, but whether it was through Mrs. Mimble knocking at the door, or spring rapping at the window, nobody knows.

As Mrs. Mimble stood hesitating, a three-legged stool, an arm-chair, and a bed came hurtling through the air and fell on the gorse bush, over the way.

"There it goes! Away it goes! And that! And that!" shouted Mr. Bumble, and the warming-pan and the kettle followed after.

"Whatever are you doing, Mr. Bumble?" exclaimed Mrs. Mimble, now thoroughly alarmed.

"Oh, good day, Mrs. Mimble. A Happy New Year to you," said the Bee, popping a whisker round the door. "I'm spring-cleaning. There isn't room to stir in this house until I've emptied it. I am giving it a good turn-out," and a saucepan and fiddle flew over the Mouse's head.

"It's a fine day for your spring-cleaning," called Mrs. Mimble, trying to make her high little squeak heard over the Buzz-Buzz, Hum, Hum, Hum-m-m, and the clatter of dishes and furniture.

"Yes, Buzz! Buzz! It is a fine day. I think I slept too long, so I'm making up for lost time."

"Lost thyme, did you say? It isn't out yet, but white rock is, and I have brought you some." She laid her bunch near his door.

But when a table crashed down on her long slender tail, she fled past the gorse bush where the bed lay among the prickles, past the rose bush where the fiddle and warming-pan hung on the thorns, to her own little house. She pushed open the door and sank on a chair.

"Well, I never!" she cried. "I'm thankful to get safely here, and more than thankful that rose bush is between my house and Mr. Bumble's! His may be the tiniest house in all the world, it is certainly the noisiest!"

She looked round her kitchen, and for the first time noticed a cobweb hanging from the ceiling, and drifted leaves and soil on her grass-woven carpet.

Up she jumped and seized a broom. Soon she was as busy as Mr. Bumble. She hung out the carpet on a low branch of the rose-tree to blow in the wind and she scrubbed her floor. She swept the walls, and hung fresh white curtains at the window, where they fluttered like flower-petals. She festooned her blankets on the bushes, and wound up the dandelion clock, and polished her table and chairs. She made the teapot shine like a moonbeam.

All the time she could hear a loud Hum-Hum-Boom-Boom-Buzz coming from over the rose bush, and a bang and clatter as knives, forks, and spoons flew about.

When she had finished her work, and her house smelled of wild-thyme soap, and lavender polish, Bumble Bee was collecting his possessions from the gorse bush and rose bush where they had fallen.

"Boom! Boom! Buzz! Help me, Mrs. Mimble!" he called, and she ran outside and sat with little paws held up, and her bright eyes inquiring what was the matter.

"I've lost a spoon, my honey-spoon. It has a patent handle to keep it from falling in the honey-pot, and now I've lost it," and he buzzed up and down impatiently, seeking among the spiny branches of the rose bush.

Mrs. Mimble looked among the brown leaves of the foxglove, but it wasn't there. She turned over the violet leaves, and peeped among the green flowers of the Jack-by-the-hedge, and ran in and out of the gorse bush, but still she could not find it.

It was lost, and Mr. Bumble grumbled so loudly that a passer-by exclaimed: "It is really spring! Listen to the bees humming!"

Except for the loss of his spoon Mr. Bumble was perfectly happy, and his friend, Mrs. Mimble, was so merry it was a joy to be near her. Although she was too large to enter his house, he used to visit hers, and many an evening they spent before her open window, eating honey and wheat biscuits, and sipping nectar as they listened to the song of the bees. Each day was a delight to these little field-people.

One morning the Mouse knocked on Mr. Bumble's door and called to him to come out.

"I have some news, Mr. Bumble, some news! I've found a nest to let," she cried.

Mr. Bumble was resting after a long flight across the Ten-Acre Field, but he put down his newspaper and flew to the door.

"A nest? What do you want with a nest?" he asked.

"It's a chaffinch's nest, a beautiful old one, lined with the very best hair and wool. It will make a summer-house, where I can go for a change of air now and then."

"Shall we both go and see it?" asked the Bee, kindly.

Mrs. Mimble ran home and put on her best red dress with fur edging, and her brown bonnet and shawl in honour of the occasion. The Bee combed his hair and brushed his coat with the little comb and brush he carried in his trousers pocket.

They walked down the lane together, but soon Mr. Bumble was left behind. He was such a slow walker,

and Mrs. Mimble was so nimble, she ran backwards and forwards in her excitement, urging him on.

"Come on, Mr. Bumble. Hurry up, Mr. Bee," she cried.

"It's this dust that gets on my fur," said the Bee. "Besides, you must remember that my legs are shorter than yours."

He puffed and panted and scurried along, but Mrs. Mimble was impatient.

"Can't you fly?" she asked.

"Oh, yes, I can fly," he replied, ruffled because he wished to try to walk with her. He shook the dust from his legs, and with a deep Hum-m-m-m he soared up into the air. Higher and higher he flew, into the branches of the beech-tree, where he buzzed among the long golden buds with their tips of green.

"Now he's gone, and I have offended him," said the Mouse, ruefully. She sat sadly on a daisy tuffet, with her tearful eyes searching among the trees for her friend. At length she spied him, swinging on a twig, fluttering like a goldfinch on a thistle.

"Come down, Mr. Bumble, come down," she piped in her wee shrill voice. "I will run, and you shall fly just over my head, then we shall arrive together. And I do think you are a splendid pedestrian for your size."

Mrs. Mimble looked so pathetic and small down there under the great trees, that he relented and flew down to her. He was flattered too at the long word she had used. So they travelled, great friends again, along the lane, under the hedge of thorn and ash, she running in and out of the golden celandines and green fountains of Jack-by-the-hedge, he buzzing and singing and sipping the honey as he flew near.

When they reached the thickest part of the hedge, she ran up a stout hawthorn bush, and leaped into a small oval nest which had a label "To Let" nailed to it by a large thorn.

"Isn't it a perfect house, with a view, too!" said the Mouse, waving her paw to the hills far away.

The Bee perched near on a bough, and swayed

backwards and forwards with admiration. The nest was green and silver with moss and lichen, delicate as a mistletoe bunch. Its roof was open to the stars, but an overhanging mat of twigs and leaves kept out the rain. All that Mrs. Mimble needed was a coverlet, and then she could sleep, lulled by the wind.

"I shall bring my brown silk quilt and keep it here, for no one will take it, it's just like a dead leaf. When I want a change of air, I shall come for a day or two, and live among the may blossom."

They agreed she should take possession at once.

Mr. Bumble, whose handwriting was neat, wrote another notice, and pinned it to the tree, for all to read who could.

MRS. MIMBLE
HER HOUSE
PRIVATE

The very next day she came with the brown silk quilt, and her toothbrush and comb packed in a little bag. The Bee sat outside his own small house, and waved a red handkerchief to her.

"Good-bye. I will keep the robbers from your home," he called, and he locked her door and put the key in his pocket.

Mrs. Mimble climbed up to her summer-house, and leaned from the balcony to watch the life below.

Ants scurried along the grass, dragging loads of wood for their stockades. Sometimes two or three carried a twig, or a bundle of sticks. One little ant dropped his log down a hole, and all his efforts could not move it. As he pulled and tugged a large ant came up and boxed his ears for carelessness. Then he

seized the wood and took it away himself to the Ant Town.

"A shame! A shame!" called Mrs. Mimble. "It's the little fellow's log. He found it," but no one took any notice, and the small weeping ant dried his tears on the leaves.

Then Mrs. Mimble heard a tinkle of small voices, and a lady-bird came by with her five children dressed in red spotted cloaks.

"How many legs has a caterpillar got, Mother?" inquired a tiny voice, but the mother hurried along, and then flew up in the air with the children following, and Mrs. Mimble, who nearly fell out of her nest as she watched them, never heard the answer.

"I will ask Mr. Bumble," said she. "He knows everything."

Two beetles swaggered up and began to fight. They rose on their hind legs and cuffed and kicked each other. They circled round and round one another, with clenched fists and glaring eyes.

"It's mine. I found it," said one beetle, swinging out his arm.

"Take that, and that!" shouted the other, boxing with both arms at once, and dancing with rage. "I saw it fall, and I had it first."

"I carried it here," said the first beetle, parrying the blows.

Mrs. Mimble glanced round, and there, on a wide-open dandelion lay a tiny gleaming spoon—Bumble Bee's honey-spoon with the patent handle.

Softly she ran down the tree, and silently she slipped under the shelter of the jagged dandelion leaves, and put the spoon in her pocket. Then she returned as quietly as she had come, and still the beetles banged and biffed each other, shouting: "It's mine."

At last, tired out, they sat down for a minute's rest, and lo! the treasure was gone! Whereupon they scurried here and there, hunting in the grass, till Mrs. Mimble lost sight of them.

She put on her bonnet, intending to run home with the find, when she heard the loud Zoom! Buzz! Buzz! of her friend, and the Bumble Bee came blundering along in a zig-zag path, struggling to carry a long bright object on his back.

"I thought the new house might be damp," he panted, bringing the copper warming-pan from across his wing, "for no one has slept in it since the chaffinches were here last spring."

"Oh, Mr. Bumble, how kind you are! How thoughtful!" exclaimed the Mouse. She rubbed the warming-pan, which contained an imprisoned sunbeam, over the downy nest and drove out the little damps.

"Now I have something for you," she continued, and she took from her pocket the honey-spoon, the small spoon as big as a daisy petal with its patent handle and all.

The sun came out from behind a round cloud, the small leaves packed in their sheaths moved and struggled to get out. Mrs. Mimble heard the sound of the million buds around her, whispering, uncurling, and flinging away their wraps as they peeped at the sun. She leaned from her balcony and watched the crowds of field creatures, snails and ants, coming and going in the grassy streets below.

But restless Mr. Bumble flew away for his fiddle, away across the field and along the lane to his own smallest house. He tuned the little fiddle, and dusted it, and held it under his wide chin. Then he settled himself on a bough near his dear friend, and played the song of the Fairy Etain, who was changed into a Bee, in Ireland, a thousand years ago, but has always been remembered in legend and verse by the bees themselves.

The gentle Mouse sat listening to his tiny notes, sweet as honey, golden as the sunlight overhead, and she was glad, for she knew that summer was not far away.

The Weather Cock

At the top of All Saints' Church steeple stood a Cock. For many years he had balanced himself on the slender spire, twisting and turning with the wind, gazing over the wide countryside. From where he perched he could see green meadows and the shining river, thatched cottages half-hidden by clustering sycamore trees, the village school with its clanging bell, and the busy little street.

There was always something going on down below, and as the Cock's eyes never closed, he saw more than most people.

He watched the ploughman guide his horses across the fields in the early spring, when the gulls wheeled around his head, screaming their news as they searched for food. He saw the reaping machine gather the corn in autumn, when the pheasants rose with a clatter of fear. He watched the fisherman cast his line into the swirling waters of the river, and draw out the slim silver fish.

He saw the babies brought to church in long white robes, and years later marry, and bring their own little children. He heard the chatter of voices in the playground, and the drone from the school, which lay next to the church. No one could say the Weather Cock's life was dull. He even looked into the nests of the rooks, and had a word with the cawing birds, who hurried home to their young ones.

"Hurry up, hurry up," he cried. "Young Jack is

leaning over the edge of the nest. A little farther and he will fall and break his neck."

"Hurry up, hurry up," he called again in his rusty creaking voice. "A thief is stealing the sticks from your nest."

The rooks flapped hastily by, cawing their thanks.

When the East Wind blew he warned the old villagers to stay indoors and sit in the chimney corners.

" *East Wind, East Wind,*
Stay behind, stay behind," he sang.

Of course he pronounced Wind in the old way, for he had been there for close on two hundred years.

And when the wind blew from the North he flapped his iron wings and called:

" *A Wind from the North,*
Pray don't come forth,"

and everybody shut and bolted the doors and fastened the shutters, as the gale howled round the cottages and threatened to take off the roofs.

When the wind blew from the West, he called:

" *A West Wind, a West Wind,*
Put on your cloak and never mind,"

and the old people put their cloaks and coats on their backs, and walked down the street to see what was a-doing.

But when the wind blew from the South, he gently cried:

" *A Wind from the South*
Is sweet to the mouth,"

and the aged men and women came out of their cottage doors to sit in their little gardens, and young children brought out their bread and milk to eat under the sycamore trees.

It was a great responsibility, keeping all the very old and very young from harm, besides warning the farmer, and helping the birds, and the Weather Cock at last got tired. He often felt lonely, too, as he watched the long-tailed bright-eyed cock in the poultry yard at the farm strut up and down, with proudly lifted feet and fine long spurs. How he envied him!

He wished he, too, could pick up grains of corn from the cobbled yard, and scratch among the straw. He longed to fly on to the open half-door of the barn and shout "Cock-a-doodle-doo" to the brown speckled hens gathered below, gazing at him in admiration.

One winter's night he stood brooding on the steeple, listening to the singing of hymns in the church below. It was Christmas time, and the choir boys were practising. The Cock knew every hymn by heart, he had heard them so often during his two hundred years of life. But this time all was different, he felt lonely and sad, and a strange pain came in his breast.

A tear dropped from his eye, and then another and another. But the icy North Wind blew on them, the frost froze them, and they dropped in the churchyard below as little balls of ice.

"It's hailing!" cried the little choir boys as they scampered, with red and blue mufflers round their necks and pink buttons of noses peeping out, down the church walk to their homes.

The Cock wept for loneliness, and the hailstones bounced down on the path below. Whatever was the matter with him? He had never felt like this before! He had never been able to cry. It was a new experience, and the tears rolled down faster.

The hours chimed from the clock in the steeple, and still the Cock wept. Midnight fell, and a shiver went through the iron breast of the Weather Cock.

His feet felt suddenly light, his wings moved with ease. He stretched them out, drew himself up to his full height, and flew out into the night. Down, down, he flew from the high steeple, past the churchyard with the white graves, and the ivy-covered school, past the smithy and the miller's house, to the farmyard. He nestled under the haystack and fell asleep, for the first time in his life.

In the morning he joined the flock of hens and the black-tailed cock.

They showed him the warm hen-house with its little narrow staircase, down which they climbed each morning when the farmer opened their door, and they took him to the water trough where the icy spring flowed.

The villagers stared up at the empty steeple in amazement. They rubbed their eyes and fetched their spy-glasses, but the Cock had completely disappeared. Only the big letters, N, E, W, S, were left. So they asked the blacksmith to make an angel to stand on the steeple, and tell them about the weather.

But when the farmer saw the new Cock with his iron-grey feathers and his fine red wattles, he said to his wife:

"Here's a splendid bird, come to bring Good Luck to us on Christmas morning; for it's my belief he's flown down from yonder steeple."

"It's the right place for an angel," said the Cock to the crowd of sympathetic hens. "He can take care of the village, but as for me, the barn door is my steeple," and he flew up to the open door, and cried, "Cock-a-doodle-doo."

The Brook's Secret

Somewhere in England there is a long steep field, with oak trees and hawthorns growing round the borders, and foxglove and dog-roses standing purple and pink under the walls. Down the middle runs a wild little brook, which is in such a hurry you can scarcely hear what it says. But all the time it calls, "A secret! A secret! A secret!"

I found out the secret, and here it is.

Near the brook once stood a tiny green house. It had a roof of green rushes, two lattice windows, one up and one down, and a brown door. The door-knocker was a hawthorn berry, and the door-mat a thistle flower, which, as you know, is a soft white brush, just right for small muddy feet.

At the back was a narrow window which was upstairs, yet level with the ground, for the field was so steep one could step out from the wee bedroom on to the grassy slope.

In this pretty house lived a frog. He was a good-natured little fellow, with bright eyes and cheerful manners.

He played the flute, and every evening he could be heard piping away, or singing with his croaky voice as he sat by the front door looking out at the stream, or as he leaned from his bedroom window peeping up the field at the foxgloves.

One day he saw something in the grass on the hill-side, something strange, like a bit of sky fallen to the

ground. He fetched his spy-glass, which was a bulrush stem, and peered again from his back window. Then he went up the hill with his cherry-wood stick in his hand, hopping and skipping, panting and excited to get a nearer look.

Whatever could it be, this exquisite creature? There she lay, half hidden by the buttercups and daisies, a fairy girl with golden hair and a dress of blue gauze!

The frog was filled with delight as he gazed at her. He made a litter of cunningly woven leaves, and carried her carefully home. He touched her tiny curved fingers, and spoke gently to her in his husky whisper.

But she never answered; she smiled and smiled, so that he knew she was happy, but never a word did she utter. He laid her on a bed of sheep's wool, which he had plucked from the brambles, and she shut her blue eyes and slept. He roused her, and lifted her to a chair of bracken fronds, and she opened her wonderful eyes again.

The frog was enraptured. He sat by this delicate lady, and played his little flute to her. But although she never failed to reward him with a smile, she never spoke a word.

"She must be hungry," said he, and he put fresh watercress, duckweed and groundsel before her, but she never ate. He picked round pearly mushrooms from the meadows, and berries, and seeds of sweet plants, and made salads of burnet and sorrel and thyme, but she only smiled.

He even brought an egg from the farmyard, rolling it downhill, pushing it uphill, until he got it, all green with grass stains, to her side. But she never even glanced at it.

The little frog loved her dearly, for she was so beautiful. He had never seen anyone like her before. He put daisies in her flaxen hair, and forget-me-nots in her pale hands, but her fixed smile never changed.

"She must be bewitched by the elves," groaned the frog, and he played a sad little tune on his flute.

Then one day he shut the front door and locked it, and put the key under the thistle flower.

He travelled down the stream, past fields of long waving grass, and ponds fringed with rushes, past rough little pastures where young colts played, and under great trees which dipped their branches into the brook,—by now considerably bigger.

He left the friendly stream and turned to the right, along a tiny narrow path which only the sharpest eyes could spy. It led to a garden of purple orchis, and in the midst was a house, much larger than the frog's, solid and strong, the house of a wise old toad. He was so old, a hundred years at least, he must know everything.

The frog knocked at the toad's door, and a little maid answered.

"Is Mr. Toad at home?" asked the frog politely.

"What is your name?" asked the maid, with her green cap askew and her streamers dangling over her eyes, for she was one of those freckled brown frogs who never can keep tidy.

"Oh, just say it's a frog from the brook, on urgent business, but he wouldn't mind waiting a day or two in this garden, if it isn't convenient to Mr. Toad," said the frog, and the little maid took the message.

Frog was shown into the great Toad's study, which was lined with books on flowers and herbs, on butterflies and moths, on stars and weather and winds.

"Pardon my intrusion," said the frog timidly to the wise animal, "but I want the advice of the wisest one, and so I came to you, Mr. Toad."

Toad nodded.

"I love an enchanted being, the fairest of the fair,

with a smiling face and eyes that open and shut. But she never speaks or moves or drinks or eats or sings or walks."

Toad looked interested. "Where did she come from?" he asked.

"I found her lying in my field, among the buttercups and daisies," answered the frog.

Toad went to his bookshelf, and hunted among the books on butterflies and moths, but she wasn't there. He took down the books on animals, but there was nothing like her. He searched among the books on fairies and elves, but although these were fair, they had not the smiles of the little person whom Frog had found.

Then Toad took down a book on children.

"It may be in here," said he, turning the pages rapidly with his fat thumbs. The frog leaned over, and had flying visions of humming-tops and marbles, of bows and arrows, rattles and balls. Then he saw a picture of a doll, just like his fairy creature.

"Stop! Stop! There she is!" he cried, excitedly.

"That's a doll, a toy used by children since Roman times," said Toad, learnedly. "Dolls were known in Ancient Egypt. In fact," Toad went on, "wherever there are children, there will dolls be found."

"But I don't want children," shuddered the frog, "I want the enchantment taken off my friend, so that she can listen to my flute-playing, and share my green house by the brook, and walk in the steep field with me."

"The wisest Toad can tell you what to do, if you only have patience, and don't interrupt," said Toad severely. He shut the book, and put it carefully back on the shelf. Then he sat down on the scarlet toad-stool which grew in the middle of the study floor, and addressed the frog, who sat humbly beneath its shadow.

"You must put the flowers of eye-bright, the little white speckledy flower which grows in the old quarry, on her eyes, so that they will recognize you. You must put mouse-ear, that silky leaf which grows in dry places, on her ears, so that she will hear you. You must put hare's-foot, that soft grass which grows in the meadows, on her feet, so that she can run. You must put heart's-ease, that tiny yellow pansy, which grows in the short grass of the high pastures, on her heart. Then let her lie on a bed of quicken boughs from the hedge, and she will awake. This was taught to my ancestors by an old Hermit long ago, when the world was much younger than it is to-day."

The grateful frog hurried home, not stopping to watch the trees dipping in the water, or the swallows flying over the fields. He picked the flowers of eye-bright, and heart's-ease, the mouse-ear, and hare's-foot, and the twigs from the quickset hedge. He followed Toad's directions, and laid the small doll among the herbs and grasses.

When she felt the magic plants about her, she sat up and looked around. Then she laughed so that dimples came in her cheeks, and she leapt to her feet. She danced round the little room, holding out her blue gauze skirts with her curving fingers, fluttering round the fascinated frog like a butterfly.

She tasted the watercress, and the sweet berries the frog had provided, and drank fresh water from the brook. She ran in the fields, and leapt among the flowers.

So the frog and the doll lived together, the greatest of friends, for many years in the little green house by the brook. When they visited the Toad, they took a jar of honey and a yellow cloak of toad-flax, which the doll had woven for his old age, and they looked at his wonderful books while he tasted their sweets.

But the nicest time of all was twilight, when the evening star came out, and they sat on the stools of mushrooms, the frog playing merry tunes on his flute, the doll singing softly in a tiny voice.

And there she may be now, for she was as happy as a bee the last time I saw her, peeping from her window at the back of the little green thatched house by the brook. But only the brook and I know exactly where it is.

The Wind in the Kitchen

Zephyr was the youngest and dearest son of his mother, the South-West Wind. He always held the tip of her robe in his fingers as they flew through the meadows and woods. Never had he been separated from her. He was so small, such a little breeze, he might easily get lost.

When the South-West Wind blew down the great oak tree in Farmer Bailey's meadow, Zephyr went "Puff, Puff", and blew away the little toadstools nestling at the foot.

When the South-West Wind blew over the hayrick in the stack-yard, so that it lay like a crouching brown house, Zephyr went "Puff, Puff", and blew away a wisp of hay over the barn and into the pigsty.

When the South-West Wind blew down the mossy wall by the orchard, Zephyr went "Puff, Puff", and blew a rosy apple off the tree, down among the dandelions.

He felt he was very big and strong, and he looked forward to the time when he, too, would frolic like a giant in the forests.

One day the South-West Wind hastened through the farmyard, on her way to the mountains. As she rushed past the barns and cow-sheds, she rattled the shutters, which were hooked back against the walls, and shook the big double doors. Little Zephyr ran with her, and he gave each door a kick with his pointed foot, and each shutter a thump with his small fist. He laughed to hear the cows moo when they heard him. The door of the Farmhouse was on the latch, and it flew open when the South-West Wind pushed against it, and the pair entered the warm kitchen.

What a noise and a clatter there was! The house-dog barked and the tabby cat ran under the settle. The table-cloth flapped like a sail, and all the tin nutmeg-graters, frying-pans, ladles, and mugs rang like bells. The warming-pan banged against the wall, and the ham, hanging from the ceiling, swung like a clock pendulum.

"Shut that door! Shut that door, and keep that wind out," roared the Farmer, but nobody answered, so he pushed it with all his strength, and the South-West Wind scurried out again. Bang! went the door, and the dog and cat lay down again in front of the fire. The table-cloth dropped, the tins were quiet, the warming-pan went to sleep, and the ham settled down to its long rest.

But someone else was in the kitchen. Zephyr had let his mother's robe slip from his fingers as the door shut, and he was left inside. He chuckled and laughed with glee as he danced softly round the table, tripping and skipping on the stone floor. He poked his toes into the rag-mat, and trailed his fingers through the bunches of sage and thyme on the wall. He sniffed and he peered. He peeped and he pried. He listened to the tick of the grandfather clock, and pressed his face to the glass. He opened a little cupboard door, and looked at the best pink and gold cups and saucers arranged on the flowered shelf. He looked at himself in the big copper preserving-pan, and grimaced at the tiny mirror over the sink.

The fire frightened him at first, but he crept nearer and lay on his face on the hearth. He blew and blew. A red flame darted up and the coal glowed. He blew harder, and fountains of sparks flew out, and the chimney roared.

The tabby cat and the house-dog moved uneasily and looked around them. The Farmer glanced up from his newspaper.

"Chimbley's a-roaring bad," said he.

Zephyr leapt up, full of mischief, and blew the cat's whiskers. Pussy dashed under the dresser, where she crouched with curved back and startled eyes, ready to spring. Zephyr went "Puff, Puff", at the dog, and with a howl he ran under the table.

"Th' dog's uneasy like," said the Farmer, and he went on reading.

The little wind gave the ham a push, and it swung to and fro, between the rafters of the ceiling. He thumped the warming-pan, and it swayed on the wall, winking in the firelight. He blew the table-cloth, and it flapped in the breeze. He went "Puff, Puff, Puff", at the newspaper, and it flew out of the Farmer's grasp, and floated across the kitchen.

"Drat the thing!" he cried. "Where's the draught coming from?"

The windows and doors were shut, but still the rattling and shaking went on. The tins began to beat against one another, the bunches of herbs flew round as if bewitched, the fire roared and bellowed, the dog barked and the cat mewed.

"What's come to things? Here's a fine to-do!" exclaimed the Farmer.

But the South-West Wind had missed her little son. She flew across the fields and meadows to the house, and drummed on the door.

"Zephyr, Zephyr, where are you?" she shrieked in a piercing voice, and the cat arched her back even higher, till she looked like a horseshoe.

"Oo-Oo-Oo-Oo-Oo," sang Zephyr, and the dog moaned "Ou-Ou-Ou-Ou-Ou", in terror. Zephyr danced madly round the room, kicking and banging with feet and arms, and blowing with his full round cheeks.

"Come out at once!" screamed the South-West Wind through the keyhole.

"Oo-Oo-Oo-Oo-Oo. Can't!" sang Zephyr, as he flung one leg against the ham, sending it Flop! on the floor, and the other leg against the warming-pan, which cried "Clang! Clang!" as it hit the wall.

The Farmer slowly rose to his feet and scratched his head.

"Seems as if the wind's gotten into this house, and it canna get out," said he.

He opened the door a crack and Zephyr slipped through. The South-West Wind grabbed his hand, and gave him a little shake. "Oh, you naughty, naughty child," said she, "where have you been?"

"Mother, I had such fun! I do want to go there again," cried Zephyr. "I made such music."

"We make music in the forest, not in a house," said his mother, as they flew over the hills.

But in the farm kitchen peace came. The cat crept

out and began to lick herself before the fire. The fire drowsed and the flames dropped sleepily down. The dog stretched himself and shut his eyes. The Farmer hung up the ham, and picked up the newspaper. He settled down in his chair and put the paper over his head. Soon there was no sound but the tick of the clock and the snores of the old man.

The Seven Sleepers

Snow fell softly on the world, covering the fields and hedges with a big white blanket. In the sky the Moon peered this way and that to find the house of the Seven Sleepers. At last she saw a little green cottage under the holly tree in Big Wood, nestling so close to the dark trunk that its thatched roof touched the low shining branches, and its small chimney pressed against the prickly leaves.

She gazed curiously at its tightly shut windows, and the door with its brass knocker, all dull with the rain and snow. Then she flashed her lantern through the end window, and saw the nose of a red squirrel who lay curled up in bed. Squirrel started slightly when the light fell on her and pulled the sheet over her face.

"Safe as moonshine," said the Moon, and she peeped through all the little windows in a row under the eaves. In each room somebody lay asleep, and the Moon laughed to herself.

As she stared in at the tiny room with delicate blue curtains, the room which was so small she could scarcely get her moonbeam inside, she heard a slight sound, and a strange being came through the wood.

His face was glowing with light, and his kind brown eyes were like the eyes of a young fawn. On his shaggy back he carried a sack, and twisted round his short horns was a wreath of mistletoe. He danced

along on his cloven hoofs, and played on thin reed pipes the sweetest music the Moon had ever heard.

The Moon bowed when she saw him, and shielded her lantern, for no light was needed when Pan the Friend was there.

"You are first," said Pan, resting the sack on the snow. "Are they all asleep in there?" and he pointed to the windows.

"Yes, Your Majesty," replied the Moon, "but Squirrel is restless."

"She always is," laughed Pan, straightening out his broad shoulders, and stamping his hoofs on the ground. "She always is. The least sound, and out of bed she hops. She is the only wakeful one of the Seven Sleepers, and when she comes out in the Winter, woe betide her if I am not near!"

"Is Your Majesty honouring them with a visit?" asked the Moon.

"Of course," answered Pan. "It's Christmas Eve, you know. Animals as well as men must have their joy. I cannot do much nowadays, but this is one of the privileges left to me."

"It's cold for Your Majesty," said the Moon, flashing her lantern up and down, on the trees and hills and distant villages, where the dogs howled when they saw her. "Shall I ask the Sun to hurry up and warm things a little?"

"Ah! no," cried Pan quickly. "I must work at night now, there are too many eyes when the Sun awakes."

He slung his pipes round his hairy neck, pushed open the door and entered the cottage.

"It was a piece of luck to see him," cried the Moon to herself. "He slides along in the shadows so softly no one knows he is there, except for the sound of his pipes. I'll wait till he comes out again." And she pulled a cloud over her face and had a nap.

Pan busied himself in the kitchen for a few moments, and then ran noiselessly upstairs.

On the landing were seven little doors.

He listened, and a smile of contentment spread over his wise old face.

Little grunts and squeaks, sighs and shuffles, came from all the bedrooms, as the sleepers dreamed of summer days, of green hills, and shallow streams, of flowery meadows and soft wet bogs. A hundred visions ran through their heads, and each one lived again in the country of his heart's desire, whilst Pan stood outside in the passage breathing happiness into all the little hearts beating within.

But there was no time to lose. He gently turned a door knob and walked into Squirrel's room. There she lay, curled up with her bushy tail over her feet, smiling in her sleep, and at the foot of the bed hung her red stocking.

Pan dipped into his bag and pulled out a pair of curly-wool slippers, white and soft, woven from the fleece of a mountain lamb. He pushed them deep in the stocking, and then skipped lightly out of the room. Squirrel dreamed of waving beech trees, and great oaks, and little nut trees laden with brown nuts, but she did not know who had brought her the dream.

Then the god went into the next room, where, on a round, soft, leafy bed lay Snake, coiled in a ring, with her head on a pillow of grass. From a hook in the ceiling hung her long black stocking, for although she had no feet, she possessed a useful stocking, which she kept for sore throats, or Christmas Eve, or for a portmanteau when she was going on a long journey.

Into it Pan slipped a green silk dress, all frills and spickles and speckles.

"She'll want a new dress next Spring," said he, as he tiptoed out of the room on his pointed hoofs, and left the Snake dreaming of shadowy green glades, and thick wet grass, with deep hiding-places.

Dormouse slept in the next room. He was such a jolly chubby little fellow that Pan stood watching him for a precious minute. He lay in his cot with the eider-down pulled up to his chin, grunting softly as he dreamed of a round nest under the hedge, with seven tiny babies in it.

At the foot of the cot hung a brown sock, and Pan put a little fur waistcoat inside it.

"Keep him warm when he wakes up, the young fellow," said he, and he touched the small head lovingly, and gently closed the door.

Hedgehog's room was next. He lay in a ball at the top of the blankets, with a pink stocking tied to one of his prickles.

"He doesn't mean to lose it," laughed Pan, as he untied it and dropped inside a pearly knife with two blades and a corkscrew. Then he tied it up again and looked at the gently breathing animal.

"That's a fine present for a Hedgehog, for life will be none too easy for him," and Hedgehog dreamed of a hawthorn hedge, thick and leafy, with wood sorrel and sweet-smelling ferns growing at its roots, and big white eggs laid by some stray hen in a hollow.

"That's four," sighed Pan, as he stepped into the next room.

Frog slept there, in a bed woven of reeds, with a

wet sheet tied round his chin. He snored and snored and kicked his little legs about, but when Pan came near he lay very still as if he felt the presence of the Animal's Friend.

Pan took a pair of skates from his sack and put them in the green stocking which lay on the floor where Frog had kicked it.

"You can skate on dry land if there isn't any ice," he whispered, "and sometime you will be saved from an enemy."

And the Frog smiled as he dreamed of murmuring streams, and lily ponds, of hard round pebbles, and soft silky mud.

"Now for Snail," said Pan, as he opened the door next to Frog's. There, on a little white sheet, lay a shell, and inside it was Snail, fast asleep. But she had not forgotten to hang out her tiny grey stocking when she went to bed three months ago.

Pan brought out of his sack a necklace, made of dewdrops, the colour of rainbows.

"Ha!" he chuckled. "Won't little Snail startle them when she wears her jewels!"

There was only one room left, but that was his favourite, and Pan loved to see the neat beauty of that room. He opened the very small door at the end of the passage, and crept in on his shaggy knees, bending his horns to the ground to get through the doorway.

Such a warm cosy room was Bee's! Its walls were hung with blue silk, and its blue velvet carpet was rich as a pansy petal. On the smallest bed in the world slept Bee, with a patchwork quilt over her furry body, and her head on a feather pillow as big as a pea. Tiny, tiny snores came from the bed, and her wings moved up and down as she breathed. But as Pan entered she dreamed of the wide moors with purple heather, of the great lime trees with golden flowers, of hedges with wild roses and honey-suckle, and a flicker of a smile crossed her face.

Pan searched for her stocking, but it was so small that even his quick bright eyes nearly missed it. There

it hung, all feathery and fluffy, on one of the bed knobs. He could only just get a wee pot of honey into it.

"Good Luck to you, little Bee," he cried, as he crept back into the passage and shut the small door.

Downstairs he went, carrying his sack on his shoulder, and out into Big Wood, where the Moon was waiting to see him again. He put his pipes to his lips and played a tune, and the stars leaned down to watch him, and the trees bent their heads to listen.

"Good-bye, Seven Sleepers," he cried. "A Happy Christmas, and Good Hunting in the Spring."

Then away he went, to carry bundles of hay to the cows in their stalls, sieves of corn to the horses in the stables, and comfort and cheer to all the animals who were waiting for him in the byres.

The Moon leaned through the branches of the holly tree, and peered at the sleeping animals.

"Good night, Seven Sleepers. Sleep well until Spring comes to waken you," she called, and then she sailed away to meet Orion the Hunter with his two dogs, who waited for her in the starry spaces.

The Queen Bee

The Queen Bee, with her little gold crown on her head, buzzed through the open window of the dining-room to the sugar-bowl on the table. She tasted a bit, and nodded approvingly. Then she broke off a small piece and carried it out into the sunshine, to the palace on the patch of grass under the rose bushes.

She summoned her Prime Minister.

"Taste this," she commanded, holding out the sugar.

He bent his proud head, and gently licked the glistening morsel.

"Your Majesty!" he exclaimed. "It is frozen sweetness. It is crystal honey. May I ask where Your Majesty found it?"

The Ladies-in-waiting crowded round, peeping over each other's shoulders, their soft eyes bright, and their delicate wings neatly folded at their sides. They listened breathlessly to the Queen's reply.

"I found it in a dark cave across the garden," said she. "There is a store, nuggets as large as flowers, piled in a silver bowl, on a stretch of grass as white as snow."

The youngest Lady-in-waiting pressed forward, and eagerly cried:

"Couldn't we all go, Your Majesty, and bring back a supply for the needs of the people in Winter?"

"Wisely spoken," said the Queen, smiling.

She rang a little bell to call her subjects. From clover field and lime tree, from rose bush and hedgerow, they flew in and surged round her in a black mass.

"Go to the dark cave, my people," she commanded, "and bring the white sweetness to the palace. Fear nothing, your swords will not be needed, for the giants who live there will flee from you."

They each took a little bag from the palace walls, and fastened it to their legs. Then they went out of the big front door, and down the sloping drive, pushing and jostling with their tiny soft feet, rubbing their wings against each other, nudging, whispering, laughing and talking.

They rose in the air and flew in a straight line across the sunny garden, over the sweet peas and poppies, past the mignonette and marigolds, to the open window of the house.

The sugar-bowl lay on the table, and a maid stood near with a tray.

"Mercy on us!" she cried, running to the door. "The bees are swarming in the house," and she ran out of the room into the study where her master sat writing.

"What is it?" he asked, frowning.

"Please sir, the dining-room is full of a swarm of bees," she exclaimed.

"Don't bother me! Just leave them alone, and they'll go away," he said, impatiently banging on his desk.

But when she timidly put her nose round the door, there was nothing left, not even a lump of sugar. The bowl was quite empty!

The Queen sat in her parlour, combing and brushing her hair. She put on her crown when she heard the rush of wings outside, and went down to meet her subjects. She climbed on her throne, and her Ladies-in-waiting stood round her. Each bee brought a load of sugar and emptied it out before her.

Soon a great white heap lay on the floor of the throne room.

The Queen clapped her hands, and a party of white-capped little cooks ran in. They stored the sugar in the pantry, and sealed it in the hexagonal cupboards with the royal wax.

But still the bees surged up and down the floor, and the Prime Minister whispered to the Queen: "Your loyal subjects want a speech, Your Majesty."

"Speech! Speech!" buzzed the bees.

The Queen rose, towering above them.

"My good people," she began. "We thank you for this supply of sweetness for the cold months of Winter which are before us. If now some of you will get the juices of fruits, we will make the honey beloved of our ancestors, the bees who lived in the Golden Age."

"Hip, Hip, Hurrah! Long live the Queen!" shouted the bees.

A party of them went off with little vessels under their wings, to rifle the fruit trees. They sucked the juices from the purple plums and squeezed the richness from the blackberries. They took the sweetness from the yellow pears and the ripe apples. Only the scarlet crab-apples and the little hard sloes they left untouched.

The Queen donned a white apron and went into the big kitchen, where the kitchen maids stood ready with silver pans. She emptied the juice into the pans, and the busy workers carried sugar from the stores and poured it over the juice. Then the cooks ran out of doors with all the pans, and left them in the sunshine for an hour, whilst a bodyguard marched round and round, to keep off the enemy earwigs and ants, who tried to dip their fingers in the sweet-smelling syrup.

When the air was filled with fragrance, and the tiny silken bubbles burst in the pans, the Queen came to look.

"Take it in and store it in the cupboards," she said, and a hundred cooks emptied it in the cells.

The Queen watched them seal it all up before she took off her apron and returned to affairs of State.

One day, when the cold winds of Winter blew, and the flowers had long since disappeared from the garden, the Queen sent the youngest Lady-in-waiting to the store-room with a crystal cup and a tiny gold knife. She cut the wax from one of the cells and drew out a rich red liquid.

The Queen drank first, and passed the cup round among her Court. As each bee drank, she smiled and cried, "Wonderful! A miracle!" and passed on the cup to the next eager neighbour.

"What is the name of this marvellous food, please, Your Majesty?" asked the Prime Minister.

"It is the Syrup of the Bees," answered the Queen, proudly, "and it has not been made for a thousand years. But it is a food which must only be used in a time of necessity, for it will not change with age." So she sealed up the syrup again, and returned to her bedroom.

Now that year the Snow Queen decided to reign in England. She brought her ice-maidens with her, and her courtiers with their long spear-like icicles. They locked up the earth for many months, so that nothing could come forth. With strong ice bands, stronger than steel, they bound the trees so that no leaf could get out, and they fastened up the earth, so that flowers and plants were imprisoned.

The Queen Bee looked from her window at the white garden, and waited for that feeling and scent in the air which would tell her Spring had come. But Spring hammered in vain at the doors of the woods and fields.

A few scouts left the palace and flew over the meadows, seeking for flowers; but they never returned, they were frozen to death.

Then the Prime Minister visited the Queen.

"Your Majesty," said he, "there is no food for the people. They have eaten up all the honey, and the pieces of sweetness we stored for them when the days were sunny. They are clamouring for bread. But the cold winds blow, and the ice binds the flowers, and famine faces us."

Then the Queen knew the time had come to unseal the precious Syrup of the Bees. She gave the rich crimson food to her Ladies-in-waiting, and they carried it to the swarms of impatient hungry bees, who surged over the palace floors.

Their strength returned, their eyes sparkled. Every day they were fed, for a little of the syrup went a long way, and every day their wings grew firmer, ready for their long flights when they could escape from the hive.

At last the Sun conquered the Snow Queen, and she fled back to her kingdom at the North Pole.

Then the Queen Bee ordered the porters to open wide the palace door. Out flew the swarm of bees, strong and well, with their baskets on their thighs, to seek the fresh honey from the young flowers which had feebly pushed their way through the earth.

But the Queen went to her parlour with her youngest Lady-in-waiting, and there she played a little secret tune on her virginal, to welcome the arrival of the poor late Spring.

The Puppy who wanted a Change

A puppy lived once on a time in a wooden kennel. It was painted green, and had a sloping green roof to keep off the rain. It had walls of overlapping wood, like leaves on a tree, and a floor covered with yellow straw, fresh from the rick. At the front door was a little green wooden doorstep. There was no back door. The puppy could lie in the kennel with his little fat body, and yet have his nose and front paws on the door-step in the sunshine.

He thought it was the most beautiful house in the world, and he was the luckiest animal.

One day he went for a walk with his mistress, and they met a pig. The puppy and the pig ran along the lane together, laughing and chattering as only puppies and pigs can, and the puppy told the pig all about his house.

"I live in a green kennel," said he, "and the floor has yellow straw on it, and at the front door there is a little door-step."

"That's nothing," grunted the pig. "I live in a sty, and I wouldn't live in your kennel for a bag of carrots."

The little puppy ran back to his mistress with his tail between his legs. He sighed and sighed as they walked home, and sighed as he lay in his kennel, and sighed as he put his paws on the door-step.

"What is the matter, puppy?" asked his mistress.

"Oh dear! Oh dear! I want to live in a sty," said the puppy.

"So you shall," replied his mistress, for she loved the puppy dearly.

She sent for a man, and he built a beautiful sty. It was made of stone and had a sloping roof to keep off the rain. It had a window and a doorway with a pink door. Outside the door was a little paved yard, in which stood two pink troughs, one for his bones and one for his water.

A pink rose tree was planted by the door, and the puppy could lie in the doorway with his nose and paws in the yard, and the roses waving over his head when the sun shone.

He thought it was the most beautiful house in the world, and he was the luckiest animal.

One day he went for a walk with his mistress, and they met a hen. The puppy and the hen ran along the lane together, laughing and chattering as only puppies and hens can, and the puppy told the hen all about his sty.

"I live in a lovely stone sty," said he, "and there is a window and a door, and a little paved yard, and at the front door there is a pink rose tree. I can lie at my door with my nose in the yard."

"That's nothing," clucked the hen. "I live in a hen-house, and I wouldn't live in your sty for a basket of corn."

The little puppy ran back to his mistress with his tail between his legs, and his ears drooping. He sighed and sighed as they walked home, and sighed as he lay in his sty, and sighed as he put his paws on the door-step.

"What is the matter, puppy?" asked his mistress.

"Oh dear! Oh dear! I want to live in a hen-house," said the puppy.

"So you shall," replied his mistress, for she loved the puppy dearly.

She sent for a man and he made a beautiful hen-house. It was made of wood painted yellow, and had a little thatched roof to keep off the rain. It had two little rooms inside, and each room had a window. In one room was a nest of hay containing a pot egg, and in the other two perches stretched from wall to wall, for a hen to sit upon.

There was a very small door, and a little stairway with tiny steps, and then a hop to the ground.

The little puppy could lie in the hen-house, with his paws on the stairway and his nose on the top step, but there was not much room for his fat little body to get through the door. At night he tried to sit on a perch, but he always fell off with a thud as soon as he went to sleep. So he gave up that room and slept in the nest on top of the pot egg. The hard egg hurt his little body, but he always slept on it, hoping a chicken would come out.

He thought it was the most beautiful house in the world, and he was the luckiest animal.

But one day he went for a walk with his mistress and they met a horse. The puppy and the horse ran along the lane together, laughing and chattering as only puppies and horses can, and the puppy told the horse all about his hen-house.

"I live in a yellow hen-house," said he, "and there are two rooms and two perches and a pot egg. I have a stairway to the front door."

"That's nothing," neighed the horse. "I live in a stable, and I wouldn't live in your hen-house for a bundle of hay."

The little puppy ran back to his mistress with his tail between his legs and his ears drooping and his head hanging down. He sighed and he sighed as they walked home, and sighed as he lay in his hen-house, and sighed as he put his paws on the stairway.

"What is the matter, puppy?" asked his mistress.

"Oh dear! Oh dear! I want to live in a stable," said the puppy.

"So you shall," replied his mistress, for she loved the puppy dearly.

She sent for a man and he built a beautiful stable. It was made of wood and stone, and was painted blue both inside and out. It had a roof of blue tiles and a weather-cock on the top. It had three round windows and a big doorway with a double door. Outside the door was a cobbled yard and a mounting block. Inside the stable was a bucket of water and a manger full of bones. The puppy could lie in the stable doorway with his nose and paws on the cobble-stones, but he had to jump up high every time he wanted a bone, which was rather tiring.

However, he thought it was the most beautiful house in the world, and he was the luckiest animal.

But one day he went for a walk with his mistress and they met a rabbit. The puppy and the rabbit ran along the lane together, laughing and chattering as only puppies and rabbits can, and the puppy told the rabbit all about his stable.

"I live in a blue stable," said he, "and there is a manger full of bones, and a weather-cock on the roof."

"That's nothing," squeaked the rabbit. "I live in a burrow, and I wouldn't live in your stable for a bunch of lettuces."

The little puppy ran back to his mistress with his tail between his legs and his ears drooping, and his head hanging down, and his nose touching the ground. He sighed and sighed as they walked home, and sighed as he lay in the stable, and sighed as he put his paws on the cobble-stones.

"What is the matter, puppy?" asked his mistress.

"Oh dear! Oh dear! I want to live in a rabbit burrow," said the puppy.

"So you shall," replied his mistress, for she loved her puppy dearly.

She took him to a field and showed him an empty burrow. It was made of brown earth, and had a roof with a little hawthorn bush growing on the top. It had no window, but there was a little doorway and a long, long passage. Outside the doorway was a great green field.

The little puppy lay in the doorway with his body in the passage and his paws and nose in the green field. At night he turned round to go to bed, but it was dark, dark, and the passage was long, long, and the earth fell from the roof on to his coat, and the soil stuck to his paws, and he could not turn round in the burrow without bringing down fresh showers.

He lay in the dark, and he could find no water, and no bones, and no window, and no bed.

Then he thought of his blue stable and he longed to be there. Then he thought of his yellow hen-house and he longed to be there. Then he thought of his pink pig-sty and he longed to be there. Then he thought of his green dog-kennel and he longed to be there.

And he longed and he longed, and he sprang down the passage and through the door, and across the field, as fast as his legs would carry him, ears up, head up, tail up, till he got to his green kennel, and there his mistress found him the next morning. Never again did he want to change his home.

The Piebald Pony

Some years ago there lived at a small farm in the most beautiful country, a piebald pony. He was young and pretty. His coat was black and white, his feet were small and dainty, and his tail nearly touched the ground. He should have been happy, for he had a dear old Mare for stable companion, but he was always discontented. His mother had been a circus horse, and he could just remember some of her stories.

He grumbled at his hay, and said he would rather have sugar.

"Take this fusty hay away," he cried to the stable-boy, "and give me some white lumps of sugar."

But the stable-boy heard nothing, and walked away.

"Be content," said the old Mare. "Hay is sweeter than sugar."

"That's because you haven't had any," grumbled the pony. "My mother used to have it every day."

He grumbled at his water, and said he would rather have wine.

"Take this no-colour water away, and give me red wine," he said to the stable-boy. But the boy heard nothing, and he whistled a tune.

"Be happy," said the old Mare. "Water is cooler than wine."

"How do you know?" grumbled the pony. "My mother had a glass with the clown every day."

He was discontented with his stable, and said he preferred a feather bed.

"Bring me a feather bed," he called to the stable-boy, "and take away this straw."

But the stable-boy heard nothing, and he put more straw on the ground.

"Take life easy," said the old Mare. "Straw is more comforting than a feather bed."

"You know nothing," retorted the pony. "My mother lay on a feather bed every day."

He grumbled at his work. He strolled along the road, pulling the pony-trap, until he was smartly whipped, and then he kicked up his heels and nearly broke the shafts.

"Take away this old trap and give me a painted chariot," he cried to the stable-boy.

The stable-boy heard nothing, but he gave him a beating.

"Take care," cried the old Mare when she heard about it. "Traps are easy to pull. They might give you a cart."

"It's a cart I want, a red and gold one, like that my mother used to draw," said the pony.

When he was out in the fields he grumbled at the weather. It was always too hot or too cold, too wet or too dry.

"Take away this field and give me a tent," he said to the stable-boy. "In a tent it is neither wet nor dry, hot nor cold."

But the stable-boy heard nothing, and he shut the gate.

"Calm yourself!" warned the old Mare. "A field is much pleasanter than a tent."

"You are ignorant," said the pony rudely. "My mother always lived in a tent."

He grumbled at his bridle and saddle; he grumbled at everything.

Then one day a circus came to the village. A string of dappled horses, a camel and an elephant marched down the street. There were yellow caravans, and a blue and gold cart in which rode the Clown and his Lady. There was a brass band and a monkey in a red coat.

Our little pony shivered with delight as he looked over the hedge at the procession. He forced his way through and joined the throng. Twice he was driven away, and twice he returned. The showman was attracted by his good looks and dainty feet, so he asked the farmer to sell him.

"Circusing is in his blood," said the farmer. "I doubt if he will ever do any good here," so he sold him.

Now the pony was clever, and he worked hard at his tricks. He had sugar in plenty, and little children brought him cake after every performance.

He wore a velvet saddle, and his bridle was made of silk with hanging silver bells. He drank a glass of wine with the clown, and made the children laugh with his antics as he swallowed it.

He pranced under the bright arc lights, and tossed his head to the glares in the booths. He lay down on a feather bed, and shut his eyes, whilst the clown covered him with a blanket, and sang him to sleep. Then he awoke with a jump, and the babies screamed with joy.

A year later the circus returned to the village. As the caravans drew near, the little pony smelled the old scents, and he felt a tug at his heart. He loved it after all! There was the old Mare looking over the hedge, and whinnying with pleasure. He whinnied back and pirouetted on his hind legs for joy at seeing her again.

He slipped his noose that night, after the performance, and joined her in the field. They rubbed their noses and stood caressing each other.

"Forgive me all my rudeness," said the little pony. "I am older and wiser now. I know that hay is sweeter than sugar, and water than wine. I know the open field is better than a tent; but the circus life and the laughter of little children are food and drink to me. I would not change."

"It takes all sorts to make a world," said the old Mare.

Hedgehog and Mole go Ballooning

The Hedgehog and the Mole walked slowly down the lane, talking of one thing and another,—the price of eggs, the weather, the prospect of a good harvest, and such homely things.

Under a tall wild cherry tree sat a woman in a red shawl, fast asleep. Hedgehog and Mole started when they saw her, and tiptoed softly past, with tiny feet making no sound in the velvet dust of the lane.

"Poor thing," said Mole, "she must be tired, it would be a pity to wake her up," and the Hedgehog agreed readily.

"But what are those?" asked the Hedgehog, turning his pointed nose to a bunch of great coloured balls the woman held tightly, even in her sleep. Blue, green, red, yellow and orange, they floated above her, each with a string twisted round her fingers.

"They are balloons," answered Mole, who was a learned little animal.

"I should like one," sighed Hedgehog, gazing entranced at the lovely, dancing things.

"Suppose we buy one," whispered Mole. "I have a little money I dug up in yonder hill the other day." He put his hand in his trouser pocket and pulled out some spade guineas. "I suppose one of these will pay for a balloon," said he, fingering the coins doubtfully. "Well, take your choice, Hedgehog, and I will pay."

Hedgehog chose a purple one, and the Mole picked out a fine blue, "like a Summer day", he said. They drew them gently from the hands of the sleeping woman, and Mole put two golden guineas in the folds of her shawl.

"I hope she won't be disappointed," he murmured.

Then off they went with their treasures bobbing above them.

"Keep away from the prickles," warned Mole, "these things go off with a bang." So they tripped along in the middle of the lane, away from holly bush, briar and gorse.

Everybody they met turned round to stare after them. A field mouse nearly died of excitement, and a vole ran so close on Hedgehog's heels that he had to turn and shake his little fist at him, for it was difficult for Hedgehog to keep his own prickles out of the way. Rabbits came through the hedge and opened wide their soft round eyes, and the beetles scurried up grass stalks to get a better view.

At last they reached their homes without any accidents to the balloons. Hedgehog lived under a sycamore hedge, but Mole lived in a castle underground, and neither by hook nor by crook could he get his balloon through the doorway.

"Don't squeeze it," he cried when Hedgehog gave it a pinch. "I'm afraid I must leave it outside all night. I do hope no one will steal it."

"I'll keep an eye on it," said Hedgehog, in a friendly voice, as he tied his own balloon to a branch of the hedge. So Mole went down his passage satisfied, and left his balloon tethered to a stone by his front door.

In the night Hedgehog kept peeping out of his window to see if they were quite safe. There they were, bobbing away in the moonlight, tugging at their

strings as a breeze caught them. If only those burglars, Rat and Weasel, left them alone!

Daylight came and Hedgehog sprang out of bed. Without waiting for shoes, he ran outside. How lovely his purple balloon looked in the early sunlight! And there was Mole looking at his blue one!

They laughed gaily, and their eyes shone.

"A walk?" asked Mole.

"Right," said Hedgehog.

They ran indoors for a bite and a drink, and then they were ready.

They tied the strings round their bodies, and set off side by side across a field where mushrooms grew. Hedgehog soon had his pockets full, and Mole found a few tasty things as well. But the little wind of the night increased, and it seized the two balloons with joy and tried to carry them off.

In vain did the animals tug at the strings, the wind pulled harder.

"Mole, I can't hold my balloon down," gasped Hedgehog.

"Nor can I," cried Mole. "It's pulling me off my feet," and as he spoke, the balloon lifted him up in the air.

At the same moment Hedgehog, too, was swept up, and the two friends were carried swinging on the strings of the balloons.

"Are you all right?" shouted the Mole.

"Ye-es," panted the Hedgehog. "Isn't it f-f-fun! Like being in an aer-er-oplane."

They were both rather frightened, all the same, as they flew over the hedges, startling the linnets and yellow-hammers, and alarming young Jenny Wren who was brushing her wings.

Then the wind suddenly dropped, and the little animals glided quickly to earth, where they sat with astonished faces and raised eyebrows.

"Good fun, I call that," said the Mole, with a tremble in his voice.

"Delightful, delightful," cried the Hedgehog, shivering. "But where are we?"

All around grew lettuces and radishes, strawberries and cabbages, with juicy snails all ready for the pot. There were flowers too, with sweet-tasting petals, and herbs to flavour the stew. Both animals feasted, for they were hungry after their flight, but Mole, who was a conscientious little fellow, popped a guinea on a lettuce leaf, where it glittered in the sunshine.

"Hello, what's this? Balloons? It's those children

again, careless little beggars," said a gruff voice, and the gardener approached.

"Run, Mole, run!" cried the Hedgehog, scuttling out of the way. They pattered through the thicket of lettuce and rhubarb, with their balloons trailing in the air above them.

But the gardener had found the spade guinea, and he rubbed it against his trousers, rang it on a stone, and then bit it.

"I was quite right to leave the money, it has saved our lives," puffed Mole in Hedgehog's tiny ear, as the gardener turned round and started for the house.

"It's a spade guinea, right enough," they heard him say. "No time to bother over balloons. If they let them go, they must catch them themselves."

At that moment the weather-cock swung round, and a wind picked up the two small travellers, carrying them over the garden hedge into the field beyond. The gardener had a glimpse of little kicking legs dangling in the air, and then they disappeared, and he stumped off to tell cook about the rum things going on in the garden.

"Got away just in time," cried the Mole. "Never go there again."

"We didn't go, we was took," squeaked the Hedgehog, who couldn't remember his grammar so high in the air. His brain was quite topsy-turvy.

"Where are we?" he asked some time later when they had sailed over fields and ditches, quarries and walls.

"Just near home. Hi! Hi! Hi!" shouted Mole. "Stop the bus!"

They were quite near the ground now, but the balloons would not stop.

"Hello!" called Hare, who had been watching them. "What are you fellows doing?"

"Help, help!!" cried Hedgehog.

"Take hold of our legs," commanded Mole.

The Hare stood up to his full height, and tugged at the little feet hanging in the air above him. Down came the pair of adventurers with a plop!

"Thanks, old chap," said Mole, politely, as he straightened his jacket and smoothed his hair.

"Why don't you carry a few stones in your pocket when you go ballooning?" asked the Hare, with a twinkle in his eye. "Then you wouldn't go so fast and so far."

"So fast and so far. So slow and so sure. So lost and so found," murmured Hedgehog, stroking his prickles.

"I'll get a few more of my guineas. Wait a moment," said the practical Mole, running downstairs to his castle, whilst the Hare held the string of his balloon.

"Here you are," said he, returning with a fistful for Hedgehog.

"So slow and so sure," said Hedgehog, gratefully.

They sailed gently along with the tips of their toes just touching the buttercups and dandelions, gently skimming across the wide meadows, and when they wanted to alight they held on to the flowers and dragged themselves down. But occasionally the spirit of adventure awoke in them, and they threw overboard a golden guinea, and sprang in the air for a real joy-ride.

The Cock and the Hen go a-travelling

Once upon a time there was a Cock and Hen who thought they would like to see the world. So they told the farmyard they were going to travel to foreign parts, to Africa and the North Pole, and maybe to the moon.

"Good-bye, and mind you bring back a fairing," said the Dorking fowl.

"Good-bye, and take care of your necks," cried the White Wyandotte.

"Good-bye, and don't fall into the ocean," warned the Gander with a loud cackle.

So off they went, and they hadn't gone far, in fact only just round the garden hedge to the front of the farmhouse, when they saw the horse and cart waiting to take out the farmer's wife.

"The very thing!" cried the Cock. "We can get a lift and it will save our legs."

So they clambered in at the back and sat on the wooden floor under a rug, whispering and laughing together.

The stout farmer and his wife climbed in their seats, and the farmer took up the reins and clicked his tongue to the horse.

"Good-bye, Mummy. Good-bye, Dad," called little Anne. "Mind you bring me back a fairing," and she waved her hand from the porch, and then skipped round the house to the barn.

"That's just what the Dorking said," whispered the Hen. "Whatever can it mean? What is a fairing, Cocky?"

"Just a wee remembrance of our travels," said the Cock, sprawling under the rug as the cart shook over the stones.

The horse whinnied loudly to the mare in the field

and then it cantered down the hillroad and along the highway, jerking and bumping the Cock and the Hen till they felt quite dizzy.

The cart reached a village and the farmer and his wife got out at the baker's shop. They bought a dozen loaves of bread and a bag of buns, which they put under the seat at the back. The Cock and Hen, who lay very still, now came out and had a good dinner.

"Refreshments are always provided for travellers," said the Cock.

Next they called at the draper's, and the farmer's wife bought some red cotton handkerchiefs, which went under the seat with the bread.

The Cock and the Hen each unfolded one and tied it round their necks and under their chins with a neat bow.

"It's very draughty travelling," said the Hen. "The wind comes through the floor cracks. I shouldn't like to get the ear-ache."

Next the farmer drove to the tinsmith's little bow-windowed shop, and came out with some patty-pans.

The Cock and the Hen each took one and wore it for a hat. They nodded with glee and admiration and their tin hats tilted and their red handkerchiefs fluttered. They wriggled out of the rug and stared at the sights as the cart rattled along the street and away into the market town.

Then the two birds heard a great roaring noise, and they peered about anxiously to see what was the matter. A red motor-bus came rumbling down the road to the market-place.

"Whatever's that?" asked the Hen, pointing with a trembling claw, as the bus hooted past them.

"Oh, that's a—that's a—er—a Dromedary, the racing ship of the desert," said the Cock, who had read a good deal of natural history.

"Is it really?" said the Hen, opening wide her golden eyes.

"What's that?" asked the Hen again, as a fur-clad lady passed by.

"That's a Bear," said the Cock, with no hesitation.

"Oh dear! So we are really in foreign parts. I don't think I want to get out, Cocky."

"No, I think we are safer where we are," replied the Cock, staring about him at shops and buildings and children coming home from school.

The cart went over a bridge, and the Cock and Hen caught a glimpse of the river underneath.

"That's the sea," said the Cock. "Now we are in Africa."

"Where's Africa?" asked the Hen, timidly.

"It's the country where black people live."

"And there's one of them," added the Hen, as a sweep went by with his brushes on his shoulder.

"I'm frightened. I want to go home," she continued, sadly.

"Travellers can't go home till the Travel takes them," replied the Cock, "but I shall be glad to see my own farmyard again."

The cart rolled along by the river till it came to a mill, and there the farmer called. The miller came out, white from head to foot.

"What's that?" moaned the Hen.

"That's a snow-man. We must be somewhere near the North Pole," the Cock reassured her, and the farmer put a bag of flour into the back of the cart.

Then the farmer turned the horse, and the cart with its travellers started for home again.

Jiggetty jog, jiggetty jog, it went, but the Cock was too busy to notice anything. With his sharp beak he was opening the sack.

"Warm soft dust for us to nestle in," he told the Hen gleefully, and together they crept into the flour-bag and soon they were fast asleep.

They awoke with a jerk to find the door of the cart unfastened and hands moving the basket of bread. The horse was backed and taken from the cart, and the sack of flour was left with the sleepy pair inside it.

Little Anne came running to greet her parents, calling for her fairing; the yard dog barked and the cat mewed a welcome, as the farmer and his wife carried the food into the house.

"Now's our chance," whispered the Cock, and out they slipped, and ran under the hedge back to the field.

"Here we are again! We have been all round the world, to Africa, and the North Pole," they cried, and they shook their white floury wings so that a cloud flew from them and made the poultry yard sneeze. Any one could see they were travellers, for they were covered with the dust of the journey, and on their heads they bore their little tin hats, and round their necks were their scarves.

"Thank you for the fairing," said the Dorking, when they tossed their little hats to her.

"You've come back as white as I am," exclaimed the Wyandotte. "How did you manage that?"

"So you didn't fall into the ocean!" grumbled the Gander, but he was as curious as anybody to hear the adventures of the little pair.

Mustard, Pepper and Salt

In a little china house, painted all over with red roses, and gilded upon the roof, there once lived a famous family. They were Mr. Mustard, and his hot-tempered wife Mrs. Pepper, and their only son, little Salt.

Mr. Mustard was a fine stout fellow with yellow hair and whiskers, and a very red face, but Mrs. Pepper was thin and her hair was grey. She flew out of the house in a passion every meal-time, and only after everybody was weeping and sneezing could she be persuaded to return.

Little Salt was an unlucky child. Every time he went out he tore his clothes, or fell over something and spilled himself, and, as all the world knows, spilt salt brings disaster. The little house of china was always in a tumult, and Mr. Mustard longed for peace and quietness, such as other more fortunate people enjoyed.

One day, when Salt was carrying home a basket of pigeons' eggs from the wood, he tripped over the door-scraper, and fell headlong. The basket flew out of his hand and all the eggs were broken against the side of the painted house. Little Salt rolled over into a heap of soot the chimney-sweep had left. It was most unfortunate! He crawled out like a black-a-moor, so that not even his own mother would have known him.

Mrs. Pepper ran out in a great rage when she heard the noise. She scooped up the eggs with a spoon,

snatched a handful of parsley from the garden, and went off to the kitchen to make an omelette.

Then she ran out again to find young Salt, for no one can make a good omelette when Salt isn't there.

"Salt! Salt! Where are you?" she called.

But Salt was nowhere to be seen. He didn't wait for the scolding he knew he would get when his mother saw him, so he seized the salt-spoon, and hurried away, down the garden path, through the gate and into the woods.

He was black through and through, and he looked like a dark shadowy goblin as he danced along. He feared he would never become clean again, unless he bathed in pure cold water, so he tripped through the wood to the pond.

"I shall come out white as a snowdrift," said he, as he jumped in.

How cold it was! Salt had never had a bath since he could remember, and the water seemed to go right through his body, taking all his strength away. He grew thinner and thinner as he swam about. He cried out in a feeble voice "Help! Help!" Then he disappeared.

He had completely dissolved!

In the meantime Mrs. Pepper's hot temper had cooled, and she forgave her son, but she couldn't find him anywhere.

"Salt! Salt! Come home!" she called. "Oh! Dear-a-me! Where can he be? Is he lost? I can't make an omelette without my little Salt. Has Vinegar eaten him, or a Salad swallowed him up?"

She called to Mr. Mustard, and he left his plate of roast beef to join her in the search. They shut the china door, and bolted it with the mustard spoon. They put up a notice: "EMPTY", so that robbers would not trouble to enter during their absence. Then, carrying a basket of provisions, they started off through the woods.

They walked along the broad path which wandered through the trees, treading daintily on the grass, peering to right and left, hunting for a trace of little Salt. There was never a speck to be seen.

After a time they met an ant, struggling along with her egg in her arms.

"Ant! Ant!" cried Mrs. Pepper. "Have you seen my Salt?"

"What is he like?" asked the ant.

"He is white as snow, and his eyes sparkle like diamonds," said Mrs. Pepper.

"I saw a little black fellow, like a crow, running along the wood," said the ant, thoughtfully.

"Then it wasn't my Salt," said Mrs. Pepper. Mr. Mustard gave the ant a crust of wheaten bread for her family, and they hurried away.

Next they met a field mouse, who sat on a mossy stone, biting a seed, and staring at the agitated couple. Mrs. Pepper's flat hat was awry, and Mr. Mustard's whiskers stuck out in a circle round his face.

"Field mouse! Field mouse! Have you seen my Salt?" asked Mrs. Pepper.

"What kind of a child is he?" asked the field mouse, munching away at her scrap.

"He is white as a daisy, and his eyes sparkle like stars," answered Mrs. Pepper, and Mustard nodded his great head.

"I saw a blackish fellow running along here," said the field mouse.

"Then it wasn't my Salt," said Mrs. Pepper. Mr. Mustard gave the field mouse an acorn from the basket, and away they went.

They ran under the hazel-trees and searched among the bushes, and they saw a squirrel peering down at them, with a nut in her paws.

"Squirrel! Squirrel! Have you seen my Salt?" asked Mrs. Pepper.

"What is he like?" asked the squirrel, pausing to crack another nut.

"He is white as moonlight, and his eyes sparkle like the sun," said Mrs. Pepper, who was getting poetical and quite unlike her fiery self.

"I saw a little fellow running along, but he was black as a thunderstorm," said the squirrel, and she tossed the nutshell away and ran down to look closer at Mrs. Pepper's perforated hat.

"Then it wasn't my Salt," said Mrs. Pepper, and she nodded her head so that the squirrel sneezed, but Mr. Mustard gave her a filbert, and she thanked him very prettily.

They passed under the alders and rushes which grew round the water's edge, and there they met a grass snake.

"Grass Snake! Grass Snake! Have you seen my Salt?" asked Mrs. Pepper.

"What kind of a reptile is he?" asked the snake, and he coiled himself into a ring and hissed at Mrs. Pepper.

"He is white as milk, and his eyes sparkle like yours," said Mrs. Pepper, shivering so much that pepper flew out in all directions, and the grass snake knew he had met his match.

"I have seen your little Salt," said the grass snake. "He had fallen into the soot, and he was black as night. He came down to the pond to bathe, and he is there still, for all I know."

Mrs. Pepper thanked him, but the grass snake sidled quickly away, for he was afraid of her strong peppery temper.

All round the pond were reeds and water-lilies, and there on the bank lying among them was the silver salt-spoon which young Salt had carried as a walking-stick. Mrs. Pepper sprang upon it and clutched it to her heart.

"Salt! Salt! Darling Salt! Where are you?" she called in a high treble.

"Salt! Salt! Where are you, young ruffian?" called Mr. Mustard in a deep bass.

"Here I am," answered a tiny, tiny voice from the water, and indeed it was the smallest voice any one ever imagined, smaller than the gnat's cry, or the midge's chirp. "I'm in the pond and I can't get out."

Then Mrs. Pepper and Mr. Mustard sat on the edge of the pond, a-weeping and a-wailing, for nowhere could they see their little Salt in the crystal-clear water.

All day they sat, and Mr. Mustard got thin, and Mrs. Pepper lost her warmth. Night fell and the moon and the stars came out and they still sat there.

The moon stared in astonishment at the pair. Mrs. Pepper's round hat had fallen off, and Mr. Mustard had changed colour, and both leaned over the pond, weeping and sobbing into the water.

"Whatever is the matter? Why aren't you two in your comfortable cruet?" asked the moon.

"Oh! Moon! Moon! We've lost our little Salt, and our home is empty and life has lost its savour, for what is life without Salt? He is in the pond, and we can't see him. Oh! Oh!" cried Mrs. Pepper.

"If that's all, I will ask the sun to help," replied the moon.

She called across the heavens to the sun, who was warming Australia at that time.

"Sun! Sun! Will you help this poor couple to get their Salt from the pond?"

The sun boomed: "Yes. I'm coming, coming, coming," and his voice was like the beating of thunder.

The moon faded away, the birds awoke, and the sun climbed over the edge of the world in a flaming glory, so that Mrs. Pepper and Mr. Mustard bent their heads before him. He moved up the sky, and sent his hot rays to the pond, to drink up all the water.

Who should come running out of the dried-up pond, but little Salt himself, all fresh and glittering white, with sparkling eyes and clean bright face!

Mrs. Pepper and Mr. Mustard ran to meet him, and took his hands. Then they all went home through the shady wood, past the grass snake, the squirrel, the field mouse, and the ant, who waved and shouted to the happy family.

When they got home, they took the little spoon from the bolt and entered their china house. They sank back in their china chairs, and vowed they had never had so many adventures in all their lives, and from henceforth they would live in peace and quietness, such as Mr. Mustard wanted. As for Mrs. Pepper she was a changed creature from that day. She kept her hot temper to herself, and only when she was lifted out of her house and roughly shaken over somebody's plate, did she fly in a passion.

The Wind in a Frolic

One day the wind awoke from a little nap under the quiet trees. He stretched himself lazily, and yawned with wide, open mouth, so that the bees and butterflies resting on the flowers were blown away by the tiny gust.

"Oh! Ho-o-o!" he yawned, again. "I'll go for a stroll, and say how-do-ye-do to the village folk. I'm sure they've missed me lately. I'll go and cheer them up, play with them, amuse them. Yes, that's what I'll do to-day."

He picked up his long length from the mossy ground, and stalked off down the path, snapping twigs from the trees with his slender fingers, blowing the leaves with his breath.

Now he hadn't gone far when he met a little boy going to school. Such a neat little, nice little, clean little boy, with his cap on his head, and his school-bag on his back!

"How d'ye do?" said the wind, and he put out one thin finger, twitched the cap and flung it up in a sycamore-tree. There it hung till the nice little boy climbed up and got it down, but his hands were dirty, and his hair was awry. The wind sat on the ground watching, waiting for the little boy to laugh.

"Bother the wind!" exclaimed the little boy, and he stuffed his cap in his pocket and went whistling to school.

"That was clever of me," said the wind, "but

he wasn't amused. I must do something better next time."

He went a bit farther, and overtook a little girl. A few drops of rain were falling by this time, and she put up her umbrella.

"I always think umbrellas are such comical things," said the wind, "don't you?" The little girl answered never a word, but held tight to the handle when she felt the wind's presence.

"Away it goes!" cried the wind, putting his face under it, and giving a small puff. Away it went, inside out, and the wind laughed and laughed at the funny sight. But the little girl didn't laugh. She ran after her umbrella, and picked it up sadly. It was her birthday umbrella the wind had spoilt, but of course the wind didn't know that.

"Dear-a-me," said the wind. "I thought that was amusing. I must find some one else to tease."

He went rollicking along the road, and the cows and horses turned their backs or stood close to the hedges for shelter. Then he saw a farm man carrying a load of hay on his back. The wind blew and blew, till the man staggered against a wall and the hay went floating off in the air.

The wind laughed to see the sight, but the man grumbled and groaned as he collected it together again, and tied it with a rope.

"The wind's something awful!" said he crossly, and the wind, very much surprised, skipped away to find some one with a sense of humour.

Along came a woman with a basket of eggs, and the wind hurried up to her.

"Madam," said he politely, taking off his pointed hat. "Madam, may I carry your basket for you?" He put a hand on the basket, but the woman felt the strong gale around her, and held on with all her might. What was happening to the weather, for the wind to blow like that all of a sudden? she wondered. Her skirts flew out behind her, her hat blew off, but she wouldn't let the basket go.

Then the wind tossed an egg in the air, and it fell with a splash of yellow.

"Isn't that a joke! Ha! Ha! If only you would give me your basket, I would show you even funnier things. Eggs sailing in the air, and dropping like rain-drops!"

"Goodness!" cried the woman. "There's one of my eggs! Twopence gone. This wind's a regular nuisance." She held the basket close to her side to protect it, but the wind had flown away to find some one else.

He blew the hens in the farmyard, so that they ran squawking to the barn, and he drove the dog to the kennel. He shook the sign outside the village inn, and rattled the shutters on the wall. He threw a slate off the roof, and dropped a chimney-pot. The wind chuckled at all these pranks, but the people frowned and shut their doors.

Then away went the wind, away, away, over the fields and woods. He felt very unhappy, for nobody laughed, nobody wanted the wind's frolic. He felt so dejected that he began to walk, and then to crawl, with his head bent, and his arms hanging limp.

"There isn't a laugh left in the world! It's a sad, sad place, and I shall go away and play with the Polar bears and penguins. They will welcome me." He didn't really want to go to such cold places, and he glanced round to see if there was still a chance of a laugh.

On top of the hill was a windmill, with great sails lying idle. In the orchard near was a clothes-line full of washing, and a little boy ran up and down, trying to fly a kite.

The wind tripped lightly to the house, and blew, just a little. The clothes flapped and sank and flapped again. He blew harder, and the clothes began to dance. Sheets cracked with a delicious sound, pyjamas seemed to have invisible legs, coats and petticoats were full of fat windy people who swung up and down on the line. The little boy's kite flew up in the air, and soared on the end of the string like a blue bird. The great sails of the windmill with many a creak and groan began to turn, and then went rapidly round and round.

The miller and his wife came running to the door.

"Here's the wind at last," said they, laughing to one another. "It will grind my corn," said the miller, joyfully.

"It will dry my washing," said his wife, as she watched the clothes swinging in the wind.

"Look at my kite!" said the little boy. "Isn't it going well! Like an eagle! I do like this wind," and he ran round and round with the wind tugging at the little blue kite.

"Thank goodness, I've found people who like me! I shall often come and see this laughing family. The world's not so bad after all," said the wind, and he danced round and round the windmill puffing out his cheeks, and whistling a merry tune.

The Little Fir-Tree

It was a few days before Christmas, and the Old Grey Woman, who lives in the sky, was busy plucking her geese. The mighty birds lay across her broad knees, and she pulled out the white feathers and scattered them on the earth below.

"Pouf! Away they go! What a litter they make to be sure!" she sighed, and her voice was like the wind howling and moaning far away. Through the air the feathers delicately fluttered, tumbling, tossing, whirling in eddies, and the children looked through their windows and shouted gleefully: "It's snowing! Look! Snow for Christmas!" and they jumped for joy.

"I told you so," said their mother. "I said it would snow. The sky was grey and heavy with the Old Woman up there."

"To-morrow we'll play snowballs, and ride in the sledge and make a snowman," cried the children excitedly, as they went to bed.

Soon the earth was white, covered with the fine feathery mantle thrown down from the sky. The grass and trees felt warm under the snow. In the wood every dark branch was outlined with silver, and every holly leaf held a bunch of snowflakes in its hollowed green cup. The great beeches spread out their bare boughs and caught the snow in the net of twigs, and the birches stood like frozen fountains, very beautiful.

Near the edge of the wood was a plantation of fir-trees all very young and small. Their dark outstretched skirts were soon white, so that each tree looked like a little shining umbrella. Now one tree was different from the others, for it possessed a treasure which it held tightly to its heart. It was a nest, which had been built in the spring by a speckled thrush. It was so neat and trim that the fir-tree was very proud of it, and sheltered it with its close thick branches so that no snow fell into it.

The little fir-tree had loved the singing bird which lived there. It had taken care of the eggs and guarded the nestlings from owls and robbers till they were old enough to fly away. It had listened to the thrush's song, and moved its slender branches to the music. When the birds went, the tree waited for them to return or for another bird to come to the empty nest, but the rain fell, and the winds blew, and no bird sat in the home hidden in the heart of the tree.

"Perhaps a winter bird will come, a dazzling white bird, and it will lay eggs of ivory and pearl in my nest," said the little fir-tree when it saw the snow, but the other trees round it shook their heads till the snow fell in a shower.

"Only hens could do that," said they, "and they stay in the farmyards this wintry weather. There will be no bird till next year."

Then they drooped their branches and waited patiently till they were completely covered up again by the warm white blanket.

In a cottage down the lane lived a little boy and girl. They made a fine snowman outside their kitchen window, and stuck an old broken pipe of their grandfather's in its wide mouth, and a stick in its hand. They pulled each other up and down the fields in a wooden box, pretending it was a sledge drawn by a pair of fine horses. They made a long slide in the lane, and glided along it, with arms outstretched to the cold air, pretending they were flying birds. They looked at the icy frost-ferns on the windows of the little rooms under the thatched roof, and called them "Jack Frost's Garden".

"The children at the Castle are going to have a Christmas tree," proclaimed Peter, pushing his wet red hand into his mother's.

"And it's going to be all a-dazzle with lights and things," said Sarah.

"Such things are not for us. They cost too much money, but you are going to have a pair of boots apiece, and that's more useful. Maybe Santa Claus will put something in your stocking, too, if you've been good." Their mother sighed, knowing how hard it was to manage. She packed them off early to bed, but the grandfather nodded his head and smiled to himself.

On Christmas Eve the old man came into the wood, carrying a spade. He hunted here and there looking at this tree and that, peering at the colony of firs like a wise owl that wants to find a home. One tree was too big, another too scraggy, another too bushy. Then he saw the little fir-tree, standing like a fairy on one leg, wearing a crinoline of snowy crystals.

"That's the tree! That's the tree for me! Not too big, and not too little, with plenty of close branches, as smooth and round as a bell," he cried aloud, for like many old people he had a habit of speaking to himself for company.

He shook the snow from the twigs with tender old fingers and then dug round the tree, gathering all the fibrous roots carefully in his hands.

"Oh dear me!" cried the little fir-tree. "What is going to happen? Do be careful, old man. Don't shake the nest out of my branches!" The sound of its voice was like a sobbing breeze, and the other trees shook their heads and waved their tiny boughs mournfully.

"Good-bye," they called. "Good-bye for ever."

"Whatever happens, I am glad. It's a great adventure," the little fir-tree sang out bravely, when the old man carried it away.

Across the fields and along the lane it went in the grandfather's warm hands, and the tall trees in the hedgerows looked with pity at it. Little rabbits peeped round the corners of the walls, and a hare stared through a gap to see who was singing the song of the woods. When they saw the fir-tree they nodded and whispered: "Poor thing! He's caught in a trap!" and they scurried away.

The grandfather walked through a wooden gate, and up the garden path to the cottage door. Then he put the tree in the wood-shed till the children went to bed. He wiped his spade, washed his hands and sat down to tea without saying anything.

At last it was bedtime, and Peter and Sarah had their baths on the kitchen hearth, where a great fire blazed, and sparks flew up the chimney. They sat on their stools and ate their bread and milk, and a mince-pie because it was Christmas Eve. Then they each took a candle and trundled up the crooked stair to their little beds, but just as they kissed good night to their mother and grandfather, Peter lifted his head and listened.

"I can hear a little singing noise," said he. "What is it?"

Sarah listened too. "It's only the wind in the wood-shed," she told her brother, and she ran to tie her stocking to the bedpost, ready for Santa Claus.

When all was quiet upstairs, the grandfather fetched the little tree into the house. The fire crackled, and the tree began to tremble with the heat, so that the twigs rustled and its song died away with fright. "This is the end," it thought.

"Here's a little tiddly Christmas tree for Peter and Sarah," said the old man. "But take great care of it, for I must put it back in the wood where I found it."

The mother dropped her sewing and smiled at her father. "Oh, Grandfather! What a surprise! What a perfect little tree!"

She gazed at the green tree, with its shining branches, to which a powder of snow still clung. There was something particularly beautiful about this tree, fresh from its dreams in the wood. As for the little fir-tree, it plucked up its courage and stared round the room, at the table with the bread and cheese, and the cat on the hearth, and the china dogs on the mantelpiece, and the holly wreath over the loud-ticking clock.

"There's a nest in it," went on the grandfather, proudly. "Peter will like that," and he showed the mother the neat round nest hidden under the branches.

"Now I'm going out to buy some things to hang on it, so that it will be as fine as the tree up at the Castle. You plant it carefully all ready for me!" He reached up to the teapot on the mantelpiece, the lustre teapot which was his money-box, and took out some coins.

"I'm going to be extravagant for once, for I've got a bit of my pension left," he laughed, and he set off down the dark lanes to the village shop.

While he was away, the mother planted the tree in plenty of soil in the big earthenware breadmug which stood in the corner of the room, stocked with her home-made loaves. The bread she placed in a row on the dresser, small round cobs, each with a cross on the top in memory of the Christ Child, and the tree she dragged to the middle of the room, near the lamp and her sewing. As her needle went in and out she heard a tiny singing sound, and she knew it was the happy tree chanting its woodland song.

After some time the old man came back with a brown-paper parcel and bulging pockets. From the parcel he took little red and blue and gold balls to hang on the tree, and a silver glass trumpet, and four tiny coloured glass bells with little clappers which tinkled like icicles. He had a box of silver tinsel tassels to droop from the boughs like falling water, and a couple of golden roses. He brought from his pockets two oranges, and three rosy apples, and a couple of tiny baskets of almond fruits. The mother and the old man hung them all about the tree, so that it looked as if the little glossy fir-tree had stepped straight out of fairyland.

On the tip-top of the tree's head, the grandfather's shaking fingers fastened a little Dutch doll with a wisp of tinsel round her waist, a midget of a doll as big as his thumb-nail, and in the nest he placed a lovely glass bird, with a white body and feathery tail and a silver beak and wings.

The tree quivered with delight, so that all the bells began to ring, and all the balls and sparkles jumped up and down and gleamed in the firelight. At last a bird had come to live in the nest again, a winter bird, snow-white like the frosty earth!

Throughout Christmas Eve the tree stayed in the quiet room, listening to the ticking of the clock, and the chink, chink of the dying fire, and the chirrup of the cricket which lived under the hearthstone, and the tree, too, murmured and rustled its branches, waiting for the glass bird to chirp and sing.

Then dawn came, and the mother made the fire again, so that the lights sprang out and the tree's dark branches reflected the glow. The kettle sang, the blue cups and saucers were placed with their tinkling spoons on the clean white cloth, and the bacon hissed in the frying-pan.

Suddenly there was a patter of feet, and a sound of laughter on the stairs. The door burst open and the two children came running in, carrying bulging little stockings in their hands.

"A Merry Christmas! A Merry Christmas!" they cried, hugging their mother and grandfather. Then they saw the pretty tree standing as demure as a little girl in her first party frock, and they gave a shout.

"A Christmas tree! Where did it come from? Oh! How lovely! It's a real live one, growing."

"There's a teeny, tiny doll on the top. Is it for me?" asked Sarah.

"There's a real nest," exclaimed Peter, "and there's a bird in it, too." They both danced round the tree singing:

"*Christmas comes but once a year,*
And when it comes it brings good cheer."

"Just see if that bird has laid any eggs," said the smiling old grandfather, and when Peter slipped his hand in the thrush's nest he found two silver sixpences!

That was a day for the fir-tree to remember. Never as long as it lived would it forget that day! It stood, the centre of the festivities, watching the Christmas games, listening to the Christmas songs, humming softly to the bells from the church across the village green.

"Can't you hear it?" whispered Peter. "The tree is singing." But Sarah said it was only the wind through the keyhole, for trees never sang.

In a few days the grandfather took the fir-tree back to the wood, with the nest safe and sound under the branches. He uncovered the hole, and planted the roots deep in it, so that the tree stood firmly among its companions.

"Tell us again," cried the fir-trees in the plantation, when the little tree had told its story for the hundredth time. "Did you say a snow-white bird came to live in your nest? Did you have bells on your boughs? And gold roses? Tell us again."

So once more the fir-tree told the story of Christmas.

"But the bird never sang at all," it added. "I shall be glad to see my thrush again next spring. The bells were not as sweet-sounding as the bluebells in the wood, and the roses had no scent at all. But it was a beautiful Christmas, and I was very, very happy!"

The Bull in the China Shop

Miss Tabitha Timpitty kept a very fine china shop in the village of Liedown, which is four miles South of East of Bedford. She sold cups and saucers, dishes and plates, babies' mugs and grandmothers' jugs, besides teapots of every size and colour. There was a gold teapot wreathed in roses for a Queen, a brown teapot with a leafy handle for a mother, a blue teapot with a football on the lid for a little boy, and a pink teapot as big as a walnut for a doll. People came from far and near to buy china from Miss Tabitha.

But one day she ate a green apple, and it gave her such a pain she had to go to bed, so there was no one to mind the shop. She called her Pussy-cat, Tibby, to her, as she lay moaning and groaning in her four-poster bed.

"Tibby, dear, I want you—Oh, Oh,—I want you—Oh, Oh,—to mind the shop for me."

"Yes, mistress, I will mind the shop for you," mewed Tibby, giving her a pill.

She ran downstairs and sat on the counter. The first person to enter was naughty Tommy Tittlemouse, who wanted to buy a pie-dish.

Tibby said, "What can I do for you, please?"

"You can let me pull your tail," replied the boy, giving it a sharp twitch, which sent Tibby over the counter into a pile of plates.

Tommy seized a pie-dish and ran off without

paying for it, but Tibby went upstairs crying and mewing to her mistress.

"Oh dear! Oh dear!" exclaimed Miss Tabitha Timpitty, "I must get someone else to mind my shop. Do

go out and find somebody, Tibby dear, somebody stronger than you."

Tibby ran out of the room and slid down the banisters to the shop. She stepped out into the street, but a dog saw her and gave chase. Up a tree she scurried, and from a safe branch she called down, "If you leave me alone and go to Miss Tabitha Timpitty, at the china shop, you will hear some good news."

The dog scampered off, dashed into the shop, upsetting a dinner-service, and barked loudly to Miss Tabitha.

"Bow-wow. What is it you want, please?"

"If you will mind my shop for me, you shall have a juicy bone," called Miss Tabitha from her bedroom.

"That I will," said the dog, and he lay down by the counter.

A few minutes later Tommy came in for a milk-jug.

"What can I do for you, please?" asked the dog politely.

"You can let me pull your tail," shouted the boy, giving such a pull that the dog fell on the pile of plates, and ran howling from the shop.

"Oh dear! Oh dear!" cried Miss Tabitha, shivering as she heard the noise. "Tibby, Tibby, you must go out and find someone wiser."

So Tibby, who had crept upstairs again, slid down the banisters and ran out of the shop.

Just then there passed a flock of sheep.

"These are bigger than the dog," thought Tibby. "I will get one of them to mind my mistress's shop."

"Hello, there," she called to a large white sheep which was running ahead of the others. "Wait a minute, Mrs. Sheep, I have some good news for you. Miss Tabitha Timpitty wants you in her china sop."

The sheep turned into the shop, and ran to the foot of the stairs, but all the rest of the sheep followed after, and there was such a bleating and baa-ing, and breaking of pots, Miss Tabitha burst into tears.

Tibby and the big sheep managed to send the flock away, but the floor was covered with fragments of china.

"What is it you want?" called the sheep upstairs to Miss Tabitha.

"If you will mind my shop for me," sobbed Miss Tabitha, "you shall have a dish of turnips."

"That I will," replied the sheep, as she stood among the wreckage.

Just then Tommy came into the shop to buy a teapot.

"What can I do for you, please?" asked the sheep.

"You can let me pull your tail," said Tommy, giving her such a tug she ran out of the shop and never stopped until she found the flock. But Tommy grabbed the teapot, and ran off without paying.

"Oh dear! Oh dear! Tibby, you must find someone better than that," sighed Miss Tabitha.

So Tibby ran out of the room, slid down the banisters, and went into the street.

A bull was passing on its way to the butcher's. "He is bigger than the sheep; I will get him to mind my mistress's shop."

So she called, "Mr. Bull, Mr. Bull, can you spare me a minute? Miss Tabitha wants to speak to you."

"Spare a minute?" asked the bull. "I can spare you days and weeks and years."

He stepped into the shop, lifting his hoofs high over the broken pots, and walked softly to the foot of the stairs.

"What is it you want, Miss Tabitha?" he asked. "I am on the way to the butcher, and he is waiting for me."

"If you will mind my shop for me," said Miss Tabitha, "he can wait for ever."

"That I will," said the bull, "with all my heart."

He found a broom, and swept up the floor. Then he dusted the shelves of china, and arranged the teapots on a table. He moved so softly Miss Tabitha heard no sound, but Tibby sat watching round the corner of the room.

When he had finished, he lay down behind the counter, with only the bushy tip of his tail showing.

Soon naughty Tommy came back, carrying a clothes-basket.

"What can I do for you, please?" mooed the bull, softly as a dove, for he was anxious to please Miss Tabitha.

"You can let me pull your tail," said Tommy, pulling at the tuft, and preparing to run off with a load of china.

Then up jumped the bull, and with a roar he lowered his head and tossed the boy and his clothes-basket out of the shop, over the houses, into a pond.

The villagers ran to their doors when they heard the roar, and saw the boy flying through the air.

"There goes Tommy, bad Tommy," they cried. "Miss Tabitha has at last thrown him out of her shop. Well, even a worm will turn!"

They went to the shop to thank Miss Tabitha. Behind the counter sat the bull, wearing a white apron, and polishing the glass dishes with a cloth.

"What can I do for you, please?" he asked, cooing softly as a wood-pigeon. "I have a fine collection of teapots over here."

So each woman bought a teapot, and returned with a friend for another. All day the bull was busy selling china and wrapping it up. Even the butcher's wife bought a stew-pot, but she vowed she would keep it for vegetables only.

Miss Tabitha was so pleased with his delicate air, yet manly strength, she kept him as her assistant, and people came thick and fast to see the bull in the china shop.

The Cornfield

It was a warm sweet-scented summer evening, and the moon and a few stars shone down on the fields, which lay like sheets of pale silver on the hillside. A hedgehog jogged along the country lane between the hedges, singing to himself his own little song of happiness.

> "*My lantern's the moon,*
> *My candle's a star,*
> *I travel by night,*
> *I wander afar.*"

He stamped his small feet in the dust in time to his thin high voice, and he felt the cool air in his prickles. A nightingale sang in the wood, but the hedgehog took no notice of its passionate music. He went on with his own song, singing so softly nobody but himself could hear it.

> "*My carpet's the moss,*
> *My firelight the sun,*
> *My house-roof the hedge,*
> *When work is all done.*"

It was a good song, he told himself, a traveller's song, and he was a hedgehog who couldn't abide staying at home. All day he had slept in his little bed of leaves, under the hedge, warmed by the hot sun, sheltered by tall ferns and velvety moss. Now night had come, and, in common with many small animals, he was wide awake, and off for a moonlight adventure.

He padded along the grassy verge of the lane, humming to himself, well content with life. Not

far away stretched the broad smooth highway, the great road to London. Motor-cars and lorries whirled along with bright lights illuminating the hedges, spinning like gigantic golden-eyed animals, devouring all before them, and the hedgehog kept away from their roaring speed. They wouldn't follow him down the narrow rough lanes and the tiny green highways, under the arching meadow-sweet with its white, sweet flowers dipping to touch his back, and the forests of soft willow-herb. They couldn't hear the rustles among the leaves, or smell the flowers which attracted the white night-moths. He plodded cheerfully on, aware of every movement and smell around him.

He came at last to a gate, and against its bottom bar leaned an old Jack Hare.

"Hello, Jack," said Hedgehog in his friendly way. "How's the world treating you?"

"Pretty middling," replied the hare, taking a straw from his mouth and turning round to the hedgehog. "How's yourself?"

"Oh, pretty fairish," said Hedgehog. "It's a grand night."

" 'Tis indeed! Where might you be going, Hedgehog?"

"Just over the fields to look at the corn a-growing. I allus likes to watch it grow. On a moonlight night it comes on a bit, and there's nothing like a cornfield to my thinking."

"I'll come along with you," said Jack Hare. "I don't mind a bit of adventure. I've seen nobody all day but a couple of magpies, and a few rabbits, and a lost hen. I should like to see the corn a-growing."

"There's a bright lantern hung in the sky tonight," said Hedgehog as they ambled along together, the hare suiting his long steps to the short legs of the hedgehog. "It gives a kind yellow light, that lantern aloft, not trying to the eyes like those twinkly lamps the farm men carry, or those tarrible dazzlers on the motors."

"I can't understand why they bother with those flashing lights when they've got a good lamp in the sky, that costs nothing and is held up for all the world to see," said the hare. "The ways of man are beyond me."

"And me." Hedgehog shook his little head and rattled his prickles in disdain, and very softly under his breath he sang his song.

> "*My lantern's the moon,*
> *My candle's a star,*
> *I travel by night,*
> *I wander afar.*"

The two crossed a stream, the hare leaping it, the hedgehog paddling in the shallow water, and scrambling on the stones and twigs. By the water's edge, dipping his toes in the dark stream, sat a water-rat.

"How d'ye do?" said Hedgehog. "How's life treating you?"

"Not so bad," replied the water-rat. "Where are you off to? Won't you stay here a while and cool yourselves in my brook? Come and look at the ripples I can make, and the waves all running away from my toes, one chasing another, like swallows in the air."

"We're going over the fields to see the corn a-growing," said Hedgehog, and the hare nodded and echoed: "The green corn a-growing."

"That's a pretty sight, and worth a journey," agreed the water-rat. "It does my heart good to see the corn a-sprouting and a-springing out of the ground, and waving its head. I'll come too if you don't mind. I've seen nothing all day but a couple of dilly-ducks, and a young frog. I'd like to see something sensible."

They went along together, the hedgehog with his pointed snout and little bright eyes, humming his song, the hare with his great brown eyes glancing to left and right and behind him, and the water-rat with his sleek soft skin and little blunt nose. All the time the moon shone down with a bright silvery light, so that three little dusky shadows ran alongside the three animals.

They made a tiny track in the dewy grass, and they sipped the drops of pearly moisture from the leaves to quench their thirst. They passed a company of cows, lying near the path, and they saw a couple of farm horses cropping close to one another for company. Sweet scents of honeysuckle and briar came to them, and Hedgehog sang his little song once more.

A young hare was racing up and down in the moonlight, and Hedgehog called to him.

"Hello! young Hare," said he. "Why are you in such a hurry?"

The hare sat up, with his long ears twitching as he listened to the little sounds of night.

"I'm a bit mad," said he. "It's the moon. It makes me want to leap when I see that bright light. Can't stop, sorry!" and away he went, galloping over the pasture till he was out of sight.

"Poor fellow! I was just like that once," said Jack Hare, "but I've got a bone in my leg now."

They reached a little knoll, and there they stopped, for in front of them stretched a field of golden wheat. It swayed gently as if an invisible hand stroked it, and even in the silence of the night a murmuring musical sound came from those million million ears of rustling corn.

The moon seemed to stand still in the sky, and look down at the wide cornfield, and the Great Bear blinked his eye and stared.

"Can you hear it muttering?" whispered the hedgehog. "Can you hear the corn talking?"

"Is it alive like us?" asked the little water-rat.

"I can see it breathing, all moving as it takes a big breath," said the hare. "It's a wunnerful sight, a field of corn."

"It's like water," said the water-rat. "It ripples and sighs and murmurs like the water in my brook at home."

The great field with the tall slender stems of wheat growing thick and close, covering fifty acres, seemed to whisper, and the wheat-ears rubbed together as they swayed in the night air, and the sound was that of the sea, a low soft talk of myriad voices.

"This is my adventure," said Hedgehog. "I come here nearly every night, just to see the corn a-growing and a-blowing, and to listen to what it says."

"It's a comforting homely talk," said the hare, "but I can't understand the language. I was never very good at languages. What does it say, Hedgehog?"

"Nay, I c-can't tell you exactly," replied Hedgehog, hesitating, with his head aside, as he listened. "I don't know the words, but they seem to me to be like a song. Listen. Now it's plainer."

He held up his tiny fingered hand, and a myriad rustling voices sang:

"*We are growing, growing, growing,*
The corn for the children's bread.
The sap is flowing, flowing, flowing,
From the roots unto the head.
We are the corn,
New-born,
We make the bread."

The three animals sat breathless, listening to the little sounds and murmurs of the corn's voice. From the woodside came the song of the nightingale, and overhead the moon and stars looked down.

"Aye, that's it!" said Hedgehog. "That's what it tells you. It's growing, ripening, preparing for harvest. It's living, like us."

They turned round and started off home again.

"Good night! Good night!" they said as they parted company. "It was a grand sight. Something to remember. We'll go again, all three of us when the Harvest moon comes along. Good night."

Hedgehog trundled home to his house-roof under the hedge, and Hare went back to the gate, but the little water-rat sat for a long time on the bank of his stream listening to the murmur of the water, and dreaming of the rustle of the corn.